The Girl Who Lived to Tell

A Chilling Psychological Thriller

by Ditter Kellen

www.ditterkellen.com

D1606093

Warning

This book contains graphic scenes that may be considered offensive to some readers. Continue with caution.

Dedication

For my children. Though my body will one day wither and die, my words will live on forever…

Acknowledgment

Cathe Green has been a huge part of my life for many years. She listens, advises, and other times simply sits quietly while I ramble on about nothing. She's helped me to grow, to evolve into something I've always wanted to be... A writer of mysteries.

Her beta reading is a huge help and usually turns into sessions of me changing my mind and then changing it again. God bless her giving heart. To say that I love her would be an understatement. She's a sister to me; a friend I couldn't live without.

I would also like to say thank you to my incredible editor, Kierstin Cherry, for always doing such an amazing job, for cheering me on, and for never putting me on the back burner or causing me to second-guess my work. I only hope and pray that other authors are lucky enough to have an editor as fabulous as mine.

Chapter One

Sandy Patterson stood in the living room of the large ranch house she shared with her new husband, Clark, sipping on her coffee and staring blindly out the window.

Today would be her first day as a twelfth-grade math teacher at Purvis High School in Montgomery, Alabama.

To say that she was nervous would be an understatement. Not only due to the fact that she'd be teaching students not much younger than herself, but because another girl had gone missing over the summer and had yet to be found.

Heidi Birch had been a popular teenager at Purvis High School since the ninth grade. Loved by her peers, Heidi had been a bright student who excelled at everything she touched. Her parents were beyond distraught over her disappearance, offering a fifty-thousand-dollar reward for any information leading to their daughter's whereabouts. As of yet, no one had come forward. Not that Sandy expected them to.

A sick feeling settled in her stomach. Though Sandy prayed daily for Heidi's safe return, she knew the young girl was more than likely deceased. Just as the others had been...

"I don't feel good about this," Clark admitted, his arms coming around Sandy from behind. She hadn't heard him enter the room.

He nuzzled the side of her face. "Why don't you put off teaching for another year? Or at least until they catch whoever is responsible for taking those girls. It's not like we need the money. The ranch makes more than enough to support us. And it would sure make me feel a heck of a lot better if you were here with me where I know you are safe."

Sandy leaned back against him, holding her coffee cup away from her body to prevent spilling the hot liquid on his arms. "It's not about the money, Clark. It's what I've wanted to do since I was a little girl. Nothing is going to happen to me. It's broad daylight while I'm at work. I'll go to the school, do my job, and come straight home. I promise."

"You're a stubborn bit of goods." He sighed next to her ear.

Sandy laughed. "You knew that when you married me. And I'm not the only stubborn one in the room."

He suddenly stepped around her, snatched up the remote, and nodded toward the television.

Sandy read the headline while Clark turned up the volume.

A blonde anchorwoman sat behind a desk, her made-up eyes sparkling beneath the lights of the cameras. *"Tomorrow marks the second year since the brutal murder of seventeen-year-old Destiny Murray, a local teenager whose body was discovered in a wooded area not five miles from the very high school she'd attended. Her killer has yet to be found."*

Sandy's throat closed at the flash of Destiny's picture across the television screen. Beautiful, with green eyes and long brown hair. Destiny had been a cheerleader at Purvis High, with plans to attend the local college in Troy, Alabama when she graduated. She'd had her whole life ahead of her.

Another picture abruptly appeared next to Destiny's. The blonde anchorwoman paused for dramatic effect. *"Maryann Jones's body was found a year later. She had been violated and beaten in the same fashion as Destiny."*

The anchorwoman continued to speak, warning the public to stay vigilant until the killer responsible for the deaths of the two teenagers could be located. She then went on to show a photo of Louann Henderson, a sixteen-year-old Purvis High School student who'd disappeared a few months after Maryann. Louann's nude body had been found less than a mile from her home. She had been beaten, raped with a blunt object, and starved to death.

An image of Heidi Birch materialized next, the latest teen that had disappeared a little over a month ago. *"Heidi's parents are offering a fifty-thousand-dollar reward for anyone with information on their daughter's whereabouts."*

Clark ran a hand through his hair. "I really wish you would reconsider working at the school until they catch the man responsible for this."

Sandy met her husband's gaze. "I can't just not show up, Clark. Not without notice. It's too late for them to find a replacement for me." She glanced at her watch. "And I have to be there in fifteen minutes."

"Fair enough," Clark conceded. "I understand that you can't simply not show up. But will you at least speak with Principal Humphreys about finding someone to take your place until this monster is caught? He's a reasonable man. I'm sure he'll understand."

Sandy stared back at her husband for long moments, her head warring with her heart. She had finally landed the teaching job she'd worked so hard to get, a job Clark now wanted her to give up.

"Listen to me, Clark. Those girls were all sixteen and seventeen years old. I don't fit that bill. I'm eight years their senior. If I didn't think I'd be safe, I wouldn't go. Besides, they weren't taken from the school. They were taken while out partying."

Clark didn't move. He just stood there watching her with concern shining in his hazel-colored eyes. "Okay. But I want you to call me when you arrive and call me on your way home. If you stop somewhere, text me your location. Promise me you'll do that."

"I promise," Sandy assured him, stepping around him to set her coffee cup in the sink.

He followed close behind. "I hate to be a stickler about this. I just worry is all. You're everything to me, sweetheart. I couldn't bear it if something happened to you."

"I love you, Clark. But nothing is going to happen to me. Now, I really do have to go."

She plucked up her dark-pink coat hanging next to the door and slipped it on.

Winter wasn't always blistering cold in Alabama, but it was this year. They were due for a light snow that morning, and Sandy wanted to be prepared. "I'll text you the moment I'm in my classroom."

Chapter Two

Sandy arrived at the high school with a couple of minutes to spare. Thankfully, orientation had been a few days earlier, which had given her plenty of time to set up her room and meet her new students.

She sent Clark a text, letting him know she'd made it safely inside, and then removed her coat.

Moving to stand in the open doorway to her classroom, Sandy watched the mass of students travel through the halls of Purvis High School like ants erecting a mound.

Most of the kids had their gazes glued to their cell phones, not bothering to look where they were going, while others held their schedules in a white-knuckled grip, their eyes wide and alert.

Not that Sandy blamed them. They knew as well as she did that a serial killer remained at large.

Sandy's gaze touched on everything around her, from the rows of shiny gray lockers lining the hall to the posters of Heidi Birch plastered along their doors.

Several students were gathered around one of the posters. They looked on at Heidi's image in despair, their voices being snatched up by the murmuring of the crowds moving in both directions.

Principal Jonah Humphreys stood at the end of the hall, directing a pair of obviously lost students to their designated classrooms.

He glanced up just then and met Sandy's gaze before making his way through the packed hallway to her side.

"You look terrified," he commented, a spark of humor in his eyes. "It's always like this on the first day. You'll get used to it."

Sandy sent him a smile. "Am I that obvious?"

"Only to me. It's easy for me to spot since I get a case of the nerves every new school year myself."

That surprised Sandy. She'd never thought of him as being the nervous type. Of course, she had only known him for two years before she'd graduated from Purvis.

"*You* get nervous? But you always look so put together and confident."

"It's a ruse." He laughed, dipping his hands into the pockets of his dress pants.

He quickly sobered. "Look, Mrs. Patterson, I've been the principal of this school for nigh of ten years now. I've seen a lot of teachers come and go, especially in the past couple of years.

There are two basic things you should remember. First, don't ever show weakness in front of your class or they'll run over you, and second, don't be their friend."

Sandy thought that an odd thing to say. "Pardon?"

The first bell rang, signaling that school was about to be in session. Principal Humphreys nodded while backing up a step. "Teaching is parenting outside the home. Remember that and you'll be fine." He turned and walked away.

Students began to hurry through the halls, disappearing into several open doorways.

"Morning, Mrs. Patterson," Sandy heard over and over as her own class began to file in.

She waited for the last student to breeze inside, then shut the door and moved to stand in front of her desk. "Good morning, everyone. As you all know, my name is Mrs. Patterson. I'll be your math teacher this year. Before we get started, I'd like for everyone to introduce themselves, beginning with you." She nodded to the young man seated closest to the door.

He lifted his head and glanced around the room; one of his dark-blue eyes had a purple bruise beneath it. "Most of us know each other in here. But for those that don't, I'm Reginald Gilliam. Everyone calls me Reggie."

"Thank you, Reggie." Sandy sent him a warm smile and then nodded to the brown-haired girl seated behind him.

"My name is Mindy Reyes. I've lived in Montgomery all my life, and like Reggie, I know most everyone in here also."

And on it went, with each student stating their name until the last person had been introduced.

"Thank you, everyone. The rest of the week we will be going over what you learned last year. Think of it as a refresher course to prepare you for what's to come. I'll be honest with you, math this year is not going to be easy for some, but I'll be as patient and helpful as I possibly can to help you pass this class."

Looking out over the worried faces in front of her, Sandy leaned her bottom against her desk. "Before we begin, I'd like for us to talk about what I know is on everyone's mind this morning. Your missing classmate, Heidi Birch."

Everyone in the room grew quiet enough to hear a pin drop.

Reggie shifted in his seat, his brown eyes full of torment. "Heidi and I have been seeing each other since the tenth grade. I should be out looking for her. We all should."

Sandy's heart ached for the young man. "I'm sure the police are doing everything in their power to find her, Reggie."

"Like they did with Destiny Murray, Maryann Jones, and Louann Henderson? You see how that turned out."

He surged to his feet. "I've been doing some investigating of my own. I'll find Heidi, with or without anyone's help." He rushed from the room.

Sandy moved to go after him.

"Might as well let him go," Mindy Reyes called out, stopping Sandy from pursuing. "He's hurting, Mrs. Patterson. We all are."

Turning to face her somber-looking class, Sandy quietly stepped around her desk and took a seat. She had a long, difficult day ahead of her. And from the looks of the faces of her students, it would likely be a difficult year as well.

Tension ran high among the students. Especially the girls. With a serial killer loose in Montgomery, no one knew who would be next.

And there *would* be a next, of that Sandy had no doubt.

Chapter Three

Sandy stared up at the ceiling, her feet resting on Clark's lap. The two of them were on the sofa, watching the evening news. "What do you think the chances are of Heidi Birch being found alive?"

Clark blew out a breath and muted the television. "As much as I pray that she is found safe, I just don't know. She's been missing for over a month."

Despondency swirled through Sandy's gut. She couldn't get Heidi Birch off her mind. "Her parents must be going through Hell right now. I can't imagine a child of mine disappearing. Especially with a serial killer out there somewhere."

"Just because there's a killer on the loose, doesn't mean he has the Birch girl," Clark quietly pointed out. "Any number of things could have happened to her."

Sandy lifted her head. "You don't believe that any more than I do."

"How are the kids at school taking it?"

"Not good," Sandy admitted, lowering her head back to her pillow. "Especially Reggie Gilliam. He ran out of my class first thing this morning, upset and angry."

Clark began to rub Sandy's feet. "Who's Reggie Gilliam?"

"Heidi's boyfriend. You should have seen his face when he spoke of her. The desperation in his eyes broke my heart."

The hands massaging Sandy's feet slowed their movement. "I can't even wrap my mind around what he's going through. If it were you missing, I would be out knocking on every door in town until I found you."

Sandy raised her head once again. "You don't have to worry about me, Clark. I'm extremely careful and alert at all times. And like I said before, I don't fit the bill for this weirdo. He prefers young sixteen- and seventeen-year old girls."

"That's half the school..."

With her stomach knotted in apprehension, Sandy held Clark's gaze. "I know. It scares me to death. And most of those girls don't adhere to the curfew in place for their protection. The school resource officer told me during lunch that a group of seniors were found over the weekend, partying at an abandoned house on the outskirts of town. Most of them were too drunk to even drive home."

Clark's eyes widened. "Jesus. Do they not get that a serial killer is snatching young girls in Montgomery?"

Sandy lowered her head to the pillow and continued to blindly stare at the ceiling. "You remember what it was like to be that age, Clark. They have no fear. They think it could never happen to them."

"I bet the girls that were found dumped in those woods thought it could never happen to them either."

Sandy knew that Clark worried for her safety. Truth be told, she worried for herself as well. But she wasn't an irresponsible teenager, placing herself in danger by sneaking out or driving alone at night and partying in abandoned houses.

Clark suddenly stood, catching Sandy off guard. He strode from the room, only to return a moment later with a pistol in his hand.

A little taken aback, Sandy sat up, her gaze zeroing in on that gun. "Where did you get that?"

"I've had it for a while." He thrust it toward her, handle first. "Take it."

Sandy's mouth opened and closed. "Take it? I don't even know how to shoot."

"Then I'll teach you."

She got to her feet, both nervous and intrigued at the same time. In all her twenty-five years, Sandy had never seen a firearm up close.

Her parents didn't believe in guns. They'd never had one in their home nor allowed Sandy to own one. She'd been raised to believe that guns solved nothing. They injured or killed innocent people. And if Sandy's parents had their way, every home in Alabama would be gun free.

"Just hold it," Clark coaxed when Sandy continued to stand there, gaping. "Go on. It's not loaded."

More than a little nervous, Sandy reached for the weapon. The heavy feel of it rested against her palm, cold and deadly. "I-I don't know about this, Clark."

"It'll make me feel better knowing you're protected."

Sandy's heart pounded in anxiety. Could she really pull the trigger if it came down to it, or would she freeze up and die by the very weapon she carried for protection?

Clark gently took the gun from her grasp. He disappeared into the bedroom, returning a minute later, empty-handed. "I'll take you out to the range soon and teach you how to use it. As long as you're familiar with it, there's nothing for you to fear from it."

Numbly nodding, Sandy stepped forward and laid her head against her husband's shoulder.

His arms came around her, embracing her in a comforting hold. "I know it scares you, baby, but the thought of you not being protected scares me even more. I couldn't survive if something happened to you."

Sandy inhaled deeply, loving the masculine scent that was Clark's.

The couple had only been married for six months — six of the best months of Sandy's life. She'd never known anyone as caring and handsome as Clark.

Clark and Sandy had become engaged not long after Sandy graduated from Troy State University. They then married at their home church in Montgomery, and Sandy immediately moved out to Clark's two-hundred-acre ranch, which had been left to him by his father.

The ranch had been in Clark's family for over a hundred years and would someday be handed down to any children Clark and Sandy might have. *Future* children. Sandy wasn't ready to be a mother. Not yet.

"I'll think about carrying the gun, Clark. Now, please stop worrying about me. I'll be perfectly fine. I promise."

Chapter Four

Sandy drove to work in a daze the following morning. After hours of bliss spent in Clark's arms the night before, she'd lain awake thinking about Heidi Birch.

What had that poor girl gone through since her disappearance? What was she *still* going through? Was she alive or lying in a ditch somewhere, waiting to be discovered?

With a shudder, Sandy pulled into the parking lot of Purvis High School and got out. She nodded to the resource officer standing next to the front door and then went inside.

The halls were devoid of students at that hour, as school didn't begin for another twenty minutes.

"Mr. Humphreys," Sandy called out, noticing the principal coming from the boys' bathroom.

He turned in her direction, his face pale and drawn.

Sandy pulled up short. "Mr. Humphreys? Is something wrong?"

He rubbed at his eyes. "They found the body of a teenage girl late last night."

Sandy's stomach dropped. She took a hesitant step forward, her hand now resting at her throat. "What? Where?"

"In a wooded area about ten miles north of here."

Tears filled Sandy's eyes. "Is it Heidi Birch?"

"They believe it is. Heidi's parents are on their way to the morgue to make a positive identification."

Sandy swayed on her feet.

Mr. Humphreys was instantly at her side, his hand on her elbow. "Are you all right?"

The tears filling Sandy's eyes threatened to spill over, but she blinked them back. "Her poor parents. I can't imagine what they must be going through."

"I know. It's awful. I've called in the grief counselor to help with the trauma that this will create. I'll also be excusing any students who feel the need to return home once it's been announced."

Sandy could only nod, as words seemed to fail her in that moment.

"No matter who the girl is," Humphreys continued in a low tone, "it's going to cause chaos among the students. We have to be prepared for that. Do you think you can handle it?"

"I— Yes, I can handle it."

Mr. Humphreys nodded and released his hold on her elbow. "If you need help with your class today, let me know. I can be down here in a matter of minutes."

Sandy excused herself after assuring the principal that she would be fine and then rushed to the girls' bathroom to wash her face. The last thing her students needed was to see her falling apart. She was, after all, the adult there. Even though she didn't feel like it at the moment.

Leaving the bathroom, Sandy headed to her classroom, nearly bumping into another teacher in the process. Though Sandy didn't know the woman's name, she recognized her as the twelfth-grade history teacher.

"Excuse me." Sandy swiftly apologized, moving to step around the pinch-faced woman.

"I guess you heard the news," the history teacher murmured, stopping Sandy in her tracks.

Sandy turned back to face her. "I did. It's just horrible."

The other woman sniffed. "Hopefully, it'll be a lesson to these irresponsible teenagers. If they'd just adhere to the curfew set up for their protection and have their butts at home when they're supposed to, none of this would be happening."

Sandy was stunned by the venomous words spewing from the woman's mouth, especially in the wake of what had transpired that morning.

"Mrs. Freedman," Principal Jonah Humphreys announced, suddenly appearing at their side. "I see you've met Mrs. Patterson."

Put on the spot, Sandy sent Mrs. Freedman a hesitant smile and extended her hand.

Accepting her show of greeting, Mrs. Freedman clasped Sandy's palm. "Nice to meet you. Name's Earlene."

"I'm Sandy."

An awkward silence fell.

Obviously picking up on the tension, Humphreys cleared his throat. "I've reached out to the grief counselor. She should be arriving within the hour."

Earlene turned her attention to Humphreys. "Is it the same one as last year?"

The principal's jaw tightened briefly, giving Sandy the impression that this wasn't the first time he'd been asked that question.

He pierced Earlene with a serious stare. "Is there something I should know about?"

Earlene shook her head and turned away, but not before Sandy noticed an underlying anger flash in her eyes.

"What was that about?" Sandy asked the minute Earlene was out of earshot.

Humphreys pinched the bridge of his nose. "Everything is fine, Mrs. Patterson. Just a lot of tension in these halls at the moment. I'll be in my office if you need me for anything." With that, he turned and walked away.

Chapter Five

"May I be excused?" Mindy Reyes asked, tears swimming in her eyes.

Principal Humphreys had just left Sandy's classroom after informing the students that Heidi Birch's body had been found.

Seeing as Mindy had been Heidi's closest friend, it stood to reason why she took the news as hard as she did.

"Of course," Sandy softly agreed, her heart going out to the girl. "If you need to speak with the grief counselor, she's available for you."

Mindy absently nodded, snatched up her purse, and fled the room.

Sandy's gaze moved to Reggie's empty desk. He hadn't shown up for school that morning, which seemed odd since the news of Heidi's death had just surfaced. Sandy made a mental note to call the boy's parents and check on him.

Other students in Sandy's class opted to go home early as well, while the rest seemed quiet and withdrawn.

The intercom in the classroom abruptly came on, and Principal Humphreys' voice spilled into the room. *"Due to the devastating news we received this morning, classes will be postponed for the day. The busses will be out front to give the bus riders a lift home. If you were dropped off by private vehicle, you may call your parents to come get you. Anyone else needing a ride home, come to the office, and we'll make arrangements for you."*

Sandy stood quietly by as one by one, her students began to gather their belongings and file out.

She understood Humphreys' reasons for dismissing school early but wondered if it was a good idea considering a serial killer remained at large. Most of the students' parents worked, which meant their kids would be home alone.

But there was nothing Sandy could do about that. School had already been dismissed.

Once the last student had cleared the door, Sandy blew out a shaky breath and dropped heavily into her chair. She fished her cell phone out of her purse and sent Clark a message. *Heidi Birch's body was discovered this morning. The students have been dismissed for the day. Will be leaving soon. Text you when I'm on my way home. I love you.*

Sure hate to hear that, came her husband's prompt reply. *Be careful. I love you more.*

Sandy dropped her phone back inside her purse and draped the leather bag over her shoulder. She pushed to her feet, intending on heading home, when Humphreys' voice over the intercom stopped her. "*Attention, teachers. There will be a meeting in the cafeteria in half an hour, once the students are seen safely home. I'll see you there."*

With a sigh, Sandy retrieved her cell once more to update Clark. *Faculty meeting in half an hour. Will be later than expected. Talk soon.*

Text me the minute you leave, her husband sent back.

Sandy locked up her classroom and made her way through the near-empty halls to the lunchroom.

Nine or ten teachers were already gathered there when Sandy arrived. Most were sitting quietly, looking at their phones, while the others were deep in conversation.

Several heads lifted when Sandy stepped into the room.

She nodded to the group and moved to take a seat at an empty table.

An athletically built woman with her long blonde hair pulled back into a ponytail approached. She looked to be in her mid to late thirties. "You're new here."

Sandy sent her a smile. "Yes, it's my first year. I teach twelfth-grade math."

The woman extended her hand. "I'm Theresa Little, the physical education teacher."

Accepting her palm, Sandy nodded to the chair next to her. "Nice to meet you, Mrs. Little. I'm Sandy Patterson. Would you like to join me?"

"It's Miss. And please call me Theresa." She took a seat facing Sandy. "It's just awful about poor Heidi Birch. Did you know her?"

Sandy shook her head. "I never had the pleasure. Though I heard she was extremely bright and popular among her peers."

"That she was." Theresa grew quiet for a moment, and then, "I hope they catch the monster who did this. Heidi Birch makes the fourth girl to be killed from this school in two years."

Principal Humphreys marched into the room, not stopping until he reached the coffee area against the far wall.

Sandy watched him pour a cup of the steaming liquid before doctoring it up with cream and sugar. She noticed his shoulders were tense. And understandably so.

Though Humphreys was a small man, he had an air of authority about him that made him seem larger than he actually was. Sandy figured he'd had to learn to be hard in order to be taken seriously. Her father would have referred to it as little man syndrome.

It didn't help that half his right ear was missing, and what looked to be a burn mark ran along his jaw on that same side, partially hidden by his handlebar mustache.

"What do you think of Mr. Humphreys?" Theresa asked in a low tone, catching Sandy off guard.

"I— Well, I don't really know him that well. Though he was the principal here my last two years of high school. Why do you ask?"

Theresa shrugged. "Just curious. He's a strange character is all."

"What happened to the side of his face?" Sandy found herself asking. "I vaguely remember him having a scar back when I was a senior, but I never knew how he'd gotten it."

Another shrug came from Theresa. "Some kind of car accident, I think. Of course, that could just be rumors. One of the teachers told me that my first year at the school. But I can't remember any of the details."

Embarrassed that she'd asked, Sandy changed the subject. "How long have you worked here?"

"Seven long, grueling years." Theresa chuckled, the sound appearing forced. "But it's a paycheck."

Sandy wasn't sure how to respond to that, so she didn't.

The lunchroom had filled up by the time Sandy and Theresa's conversation ended.

Principal Humphreys set his coffee cup down and waved a thin, dark-haired woman to his side. "For those of you who weren't here last year, this is our grief counselor, Mrs. Tate. She'll be working with us for a few weeks, helping where she can with the students affected by Heidi's death. She's also available to the faculty, if any of you find yourselves in need of her help."

The rest of the hour was spent with Mrs. Tate talking about protocol and signs to look for in students unable to cope with Heidi's death.

Sandy's cell phone vibrated in her purse. She reached inside and flipped the phone over. A text from Clark appeared across the screen.

Have you left yet?

Touching the message with her thumb to open it, Sandy sent back a response. *Still here. Leaving soon.*

She released the cell phone and returned her attention to the grief counselor, who was just wrapping up her speech.

"If you have any questions, I can be reached by phone or at my temporary desk in the guidance counselor's office."

Once dismissed, everyone began gathering their belongings and heading toward the door.

Theresa stopped Sandy by placing her hand on Sandy's arm. "I'll walk you out."

Sandy could only nod, as declining would seem rude. Besides, it didn't hurt to have the PE coach walk her out. Truth be told, it made her feel safer.

Neither of them spoke until they arrived at Sandy's car.

"Thank you." Sandy unlocked her door. "I appreciate you looking out for me."

"Don't mention it. I'll see you tomorrow." Theresa strode away.

Chapter Six

After removing her jacket and tossing her purse onto the passenger seat, Sandy cranked the car and sent Clark a text. *On my way home.*

See you soon, Clark responded almost immediately.

Sandy switched on the radio before leaving the parking lot, only to turn up the volume when she realized the news station spoke of Heidi Birch.

"The remains of a young girl discovered late last night have been identified as seventeen-year-old Heidi Birch who went missing more than a month ago. Her body was found in a wooded area near Highway 31, less than ten miles from her family home. Details of the case have not been released as of yet."

The news reporter continued speaking, but Sandy no longer listened. Her mind had drifted to poor Reggie's and Heidi's parents.

To lose a child in any fashion had to be devastating, but to lose one the way the Birches had lost their daughter would no doubt cripple them emotionally for life. Heidi had been murdered.

Sandy pulled into the drive of the two-hundred-acre ranch she shared with Clark, her heart still heavy with grief.

Who could do such a thing? What kind of a person could take another's life and then dump their body in the woods like unwanted garbage? Were serial killers simply born evil, or were they somehow created — a product of their own raising?

None of it made sense to Sandy. She couldn't imagine hurting another human being, let alone a young girl with her whole life ahead of her. Not only had someone snuffed out Heidi's life, but they'd ruined her family's lives as well.

"Are you going to sit out here all afternoon, or are you coming inside?" Clark joked from the other side of Sandy's car window.

She'd been so caught up in her thoughts, she didn't recall parking.

Switching off the engine, she grabbed her purse and jacket as Clark opened her car door. "Sorry, I must have been lost in thought."

"I'd say. I waved at you when you pulled up, but it was obvious you didn't see me."

Sandy closed and locked her car door. "I was just listening to the news about Heidi Birch, wondering how someone could have done such a thing to her. She was so young, Clark."

"I know. It's terrible. And the media is having a field day with it. They're like sharks in a frenzy, circling a wounded fish. I sure hope her parents aren't watching."

Sandy walked alongside her husband to the front door of their ranch-style home. "I doubt they've seen much of it. They're likely too busy making burial arrangements."

"How did your class handle the news?" Clark opened the door for his wife.

"Some handled it better than others. Reggie is the one I'm most worried about."

"Reggie?"

Sandy set her purse on the coffee table and stepped out of her high heels. "You know, the kid I told you about."

When Clark stared back at her with a blank look, she tried again. "The boyfriend. Heidi's boyfriend."

"Ohhhh, yes, I remember. He must have taken it pretty hard."

Sandy rubbed at her now throbbing temples. "I'm sure he is. He wasn't at school today."

A flicker of sadness appeared in Clark's hazel-colored eyes. "Poor kid."

"Yeah. Although, I can't imagine how he knew of Heidi's death so soon. I mean, her parents hadn't even identified her before the first bell rang this morning."

A small indention appeared between Clark's eyes. "Maybe her parents called his parents? Who knows. I just hope the kid will be okay."

"Me too," Sandy admitted in a soft voice. "I'm going to go take a hot bath. I'm starting to develop a headache."

Clark brushed his fingertips along her cheek. "Want some company?"

Though Sandy would love nothing more than to share a bath with her handsome husband, she needed time to decompress. "Take a raincheck?"

"Of course. I'll order us a pizza while you soak."

Standing on tiptoes, Sandy kissed her husband's sexy lips. "Why are you always so good to me?"

"That's simple. Because I love you more than air."

"I love you too, Clark."

"Are you sure you don't want me to join you? We can put the pizza on the back burner."

Sandy laughed for the first time that day. "Maybe later, stud."

He playfully swatted her on the behind. "Then off with you before I toss you over my shoulder and take you to bed."

"I'll make you a deal," she teased, backing out of his reach. "After my bath and a few slices of pizza, let's turn off our phones and go to bed early. I could really use the distraction, and I can't think of a better one than lying in my handsome husband's arms."

"Deal."

Chapter Seven

The next few days were tense around Purvis High School. Between the students' nervous behavior and the parents afraid to send their kids to school, not much work got done.

Sandy glanced at Reggie's empty desk once again. He hadn't been to school since the news of Heidi's body being found in that clearing.

Opening the drawer to her desk, Sandy flipped through the emergency cards until she found Reginald Gilliam's. According to the information there, Reggie lived with his father, Clive Gilliam.

She sought out Clive's phone number, grabbed up her cell, and excused herself to the hall.

"This better be good," a man growled, picking up on the third ring.

Sandy nervously cleared her throat. "Mr. Gilliam? Clive Gilliam?"

"Speaking," he snapped, sending Sandy's already frayed nerves into orbit. She'd always hated confrontation, be it in person or by phone.

"Hi, Mr. Gilliam. This is Sandy Patterson, Reggie's math teacher. I was just wanting to check on him, see how he's doing. I'm sure he's taking Heidi's death pretty hard."

A long pause ensued, and then, "Why don't you ask him how he's doing? I'm sure you see him more than I do."

That bit of information caught Sandy off guard. "Well, Mr. Gilliam, I would ask him, but he hasn't been to school in three days."

"Three days?" Gilliam practically snarled. "Well, I haven't seen him since Sunday."

Sandy's breath caught. "Since Sunday?"

"Look, lady. I work nights, which means I'm asleep when that boy gets up in the mornings. He's never been one to skip school before. Not that I know of anyway."

Not trusting her voice, Sandy took several deep breaths to keep from laying into Reggie's pitiful excuse for a father and losing her job over it. "Perhaps you should call the police," she found herself suggesting instead.

A loud sigh came through the line. "I reckon I'll do that. But they probably won't do anything. He'll be eighteen in a month."

"Is there a possibility he ran away?"

Another sigh echoed in her ear. "Hold on and I'll check."

From the sound of Clive Gilliam's voice, Sandy was beginning to wonder if Reggie had indeed run away. She recalled the small purple bruise under his eye on the first day of school.

A rustling noise coming through the line told Sandy that Clive had returned. "His stuff's still in his room. All his clothes are still folded up in his drawers, but his books are gone."

"His schoolbooks are missing?"

"Yeah, his backpack is gone, the one he carries to school."

Sandy paced the hall outside her classroom door. "How does Reggie normally get to school?"

"He walks," Clive murmured absently. "We only live a mile from the school, and the bus won't pick kids up if they live inside a two-mile radius."

"I really think you should notify the authorities, Mr. Gilliam. I realize he's almost eighteen, but you said he doesn't skip school, and with his backpack being the only thing that's missing..." Her voice trailed off as dozens of scenarios spun through her head.

"I'm calling them now," Clive announced before ending the call.

Sandy made sure her phone was on silent and then returned to her classroom with a heavy heart.

Reggie Gilliam hadn't been seen in three days. What kind of parent didn't check on their own child? How long would it have taken Clive to realize his son was gone if Sandy hadn't called?

Sandy attempted to shake off her anger at Reggie's father for his blatant neglect of his son.

She needed to talk to the principal about Reggie. Even though the bell would ring soon, signaling a class change, she decided to risk it. She found Humphries in his office behind his desk.

"He hasn't been seen in three days?" Jonah Humphreys repeated, a worried look on his face. "We've never had any problems with Reginald that I can recall."

Sandy ran a hand through her long dark hair. "His father didn't seem too concerned about the news. I mean, how can a parent not know their child was missing?"

"You'd be surprised at how much that actually goes on. I'll call Detective Overton with the Montgomery Police Department and see if the father has called in a missing person's report. If not, I'll let them know about Reginald's disappearance."

Dizziness suddenly swept over Sandy. She had to grab on to the edge of Humphreys' desk to keep upright.

"Are you all right? Mrs. Patterson?"

Sandy absently nodded. "What if Reggie somehow ended up in the hands of the killer running loose in Montgomery?"

"I doubt that," Humphreys assured her. "He's not the right gender for that creep."

"I hope you're right..."

The rest of the day went by in a flurry of high school kids racing to their next class and griping about how much they hated it.

Not that Sandy didn't remember what it was like to be in high school; she did. And being a teenager meant that texting, gaming, partying, and sleeping were priorities. Anything but school. Especially a school where they didn't feel safe.

Chapter Eight

A knock sounded on Sandy's classroom door the following day. She looked up in time to see Mr. Humphreys' face at the long, narrow pane of glass situated vertically along the side of the door.

Glancing at her class to be sure they were working, Sandy quietly got up, trailed across the room, and stepped into the hall where Humphreys stood next to a uniformed officer.

"Mrs. Patterson?" Humphreys began. "This is Detective Overton with the Montgomery Police Department. He'd like to ask you some questions."

Overton extended his hand, which Sandy promptly accepted. "It's nice to meet you. Is this about Reggie Gilliam?"

The detective nodded, releasing her hand. "His father reported him missing yesterday. One of the bus drivers recalls seeing him early Monday morning, walking toward the school with his backpack."

"He never showed up for class," Sandy informed the officer. "He hasn't been to class since the day before we were notified about Heidi Birch."

Overton pulled out a pad and pen from his shirt pocket. He flipped open a few pages and then pierced Sandy with a serious look. "The FBI is already looking into this, but I'd like to ask you a few questions of my own. Did you notice anything out of the ordinary with Reginald the last time you saw him?"

Sandy thought for a moment. "He introduced himself to the class. He voiced his feelings about Heidi Birch, said they had been seeing each other since tenth grade, and he felt the police were not doing their job."

Realizing what she'd said, Sandy amended, "His words, not mine."

And then she remembered something else. "He also had a bruise beneath one of his eyes. It looked like it had been there a couple of days."

Overton wrote some things in the pad he held. "Did you ask him about the bruise?"

"I didn't. I figured he'd been in a fight or something. You know how kids are these days."

The detective nodded. "I do. Is there anything else you recall that stood out with him?"

"Just that he was upset about Heidi. He said he'd been doing some investigating of his own, and then he ran from the room. I haven't seen him since."

Overton paused in his writing. "He didn't mention what kind of investigating?"

"He didn't. I'm sorry I couldn't be more help. But that's all I know."

The detective closed his pad and replaced it with the pen in his shirt pocket. "Thank you, Mrs. Patterson. We'll let you know if we have any more questions."

"What about Reggie's mother?" Sandy blurted when the detective turned to leave.

But it was Humphreys who answered. "Mrs. Gilliam died from cancer when Reginald was in elementary school. I think he was around nine or ten at the time."

Sandy's heart ached for Reggie. Not only had he lost his mother at a tender age, but he'd also lost his girlfriend of two years as well. "That's terrible."

"As for the bruise beneath his eye," Humphreys went on to say, "I'd be willing to bet that came from the boy's father."

Overton narrowed his eyes. "What makes you say that?"

Humphreys held the detective's gaze. "Because it's not the first time that kid has come to school with bruises."

"Did you report it?" Overton asked in a low tone.

Humphreys nodded. "I did, but Reginald denied it. Claimed he'd been jumped in town while walking to the store."

Overton retrieved his pad once more and wrote that information down. "And you didn't believe him?"

"I didn't," Humphreys admitted. "I've been in the school system long enough to recognize the signs of a bad homelife. Don't get me wrong. Reginald is a good student, doesn't cause trouble, and his grades are up to par. He was held back in elementary school the year his mother died. But that had more to do with his grieving than his ability to do the work. He's a smart kid."

Sandy stood there, listening to the two men discuss Reggie, when the bell suddenly rang. "I have to go. Let me know if there's anything I can do." She hurried back inside her classroom.

So, Reggie was possibly being abused at home, she thought, watching her students gather their things to change classes. Did Clive have something to do with Reggie's disappearance?

She thought about Reggie's last words to her. *"I've been doing some investigating of my own. I'll find Heidi, with or without anyone's help."*

Had Reggie somehow stumbled onto something to do with Heidi's murder?

A sinking feeling settled in Sandy's gut. She prayed that nothing had happened to Reggie and he would turn up soon.

But what if his father had done something to him? Or worse, what if Clive Gilliam were actually the serial killer the FBI sought after?

Sandy shook her head at the direction of her thoughts. She'd obviously read too many thrillers on the subject, and now her imagination was running wild.

Chapter Nine

Sandy spent her lunch hour in the teachers' lounge, unable to get Reggie off her mind.

Theresa, the PE coach, sat at a table to Sandy's right, deep in conversation with the history teacher, Earlene Freedman. The two women spoke too low for Sandy to hear their words, but from the looks on their faces, she knew it to be serious.

Sandy wasn't sure how she felt about Freedman. The woman was a first-class gossip with a side of goodie-two-shoes.

Another teacher who Sandy knew as Miss Baker ate alone in the corner, her gaze shifty and alert. Not that Sandy blamed her. She felt more than a little nervous herself. Especially knowing a serial killer in Montgomery remained at large.

Sandy had noticed the woman always ate alone, only speaking when spoken to. From what Sandy could gather, Miss Baker had never been married, had no social media presence, and was never seen wearing pants. In fact, she wore the same type of dress every day, only with different patterns.

Sandy wondered how on earth Miss Baker had ended up teaching eleventh-grade English when she was obviously an introvert with no social skills.

Several more teachers were scattered throughout the room, eating in silence, their somber expressions a testament to their obvious fears.

And everyone avoided the grief counselor, Mrs. Tate, like the plague. She'd apparently been called in two years earlier when the first girl had turned up dead. Sandy had no idea what had gone on to make the entire high school staff steer clear of the woman, but she'd be willing to bet ole tale-toting Freedman would know and would be all too happy to share that knowledge.

Principal Humphreys suddenly stepped into the room, his face pale and drawn. "May I have your attention, please?"

Everyone looked up from whatever food rested in front of them, their wary eyes holding silent questions.

After a brief hesitation, Humphreys dropped the mother of all bombs. "Another student of this high school has been reported missing."

Collective gasps went up around the room.

"Who?" Theresa asked, her expression oddly blank.

"Rhonda Shivers. A sixteen-year-old junior. According to her parents, she didn't come home from school yesterday."

The introverted teacher sitting alone in the room began to softly cry.

Humphreys shifted his gaze to Miss Baker. "You have her for the last class of the day, don't you?"

All heads swung in Miss Baker's direction. The woman nodded, plucked up a napkin lying on the table, and wiped at her eyes.

"Did she mention anything to you about going somewhere after school yesterday?" Humphreys pressed.

Miss Baker simply shook her head and lowered her gaze.

Sandy faced the principal. "She just vanished after school? Does she ride the bus, walk—"

"She's a car rider," Humphrey's interrupted. "Her car was found in a fast food parking lot early this morning. Her purse and cell phone locked inside."

Freedman, of course, spoke up. "She probably went out with her boyfriend and had too much to drink. I bet she'll turn up after she's sobered up."

"Rhonda doesn't party," the introverted teacher quietly demanded.

All heads swung back in her direction.

Miss Baker fidgeted with the napkin she held. "She attends the same church as me. She's a devout Christian. She—she just wouldn't."

No one spoke for several seconds, and then Mr. Humphreys squared his narrow shoulders, straightened his tie, and turned back toward the door. "I'll be sure to keep everyone abreast on the situation as I learn it. In the meantime, the FBI has suggested the police department send us a couple of officers to patrol the school. At least until…" His words tapered off, and he stepped quietly from the room.

Of course, he didn't have to finish his sentence. Everyone in that teachers' lounge knew exactly what he'd left hanging in the air upon his departure. *Until the serial killer had been caught.*

* * * *

About to head home, Sandy sent to Clark. *Sorry for being late texting. Explain when I get home.*

Drive safe. I love you, Clark responded within seconds.

Love you back. Sandy smiled and placed her phone in her purse. She had to be the luckiest woman alive. Not only was Clark a hard worker and a great husband, but he was also her friend, a companion she couldn't wait to spend the rest of forever with.

At thirty-five, Clark was already ten years his wife's senior. He wanted children, as did Sandy, but she preferred to put it off for a few years.

Clark had pointed out that if they waited five more years to begin having children, he would be at least forty. Not that forty was old in Sandy's opinion, but Clark felt differently.

What she had yet to mention to Clark was that her period was more than a week late, which meant there was a chance she had already conceived.

Heat flushed her face, and anxiety knotted her stomach. She prayed that her menstrual cycle had simply been thrown off due to stress over starting a new job or to worry over a serial killer being in their midst.

With a shaky sigh, Sandy made a mental note to swing by the drugstore on her way home and pick up a pregnancy test.

She left her classroom, nearly running into the principal and a group of teachers gathered in the hall.

"Excuse me," Sandy muttered, moving to step around them. Dizziness abruptly overcame her once more, sending her swaying on her feet and reaching for the wall.

The large group was instantly at her side. "Are you all right?" Humphreys grabbed on to her arm to steady her.

Sandy couldn't answer with the off-balance sensation rocking her head.

"You look awfully pale," Theresa informed her, concern lining her voice. "Maybe you should sit down."

Humphreys quickly agreed, leading Sandy back to her classroom to sit at her desk. "Would someone please get her some water?"

Sandy was more than a little embarrassed by the unwanted attention from the room's occupants. She held up a hand. "I'm fine. Truly. Just got a little dizzy is all."

"Are you coming down with something?" The question came from the grief counselor, Mrs. Tate.

Sandy shook her head, which only brought on more dizziness. "I think I'll take that water after all."

"I'll get it," Mrs. Tate offered, hurrying from the room.

Earlene Freedman, the school gossip, stepped forward. "You're not pregnant, are you?"

Sandy's gaze lifted. She opened her mouth to inform the gossip that it really wasn't her business if she were pregnant or not, but the words didn't come. Instead, she found herself saying, "I was wondering the same thing myself."

"Everyone, back up and give her some room," Humphreys ordered the small crowd. "I'm sure she could use some air."

Mrs. Tate returned with the water, which Sandy accepted with a weak nod and a thanks.

After taking several sips of the cool liquid, Sandy set the cup on her desk. "I appreciate everyone's concern, but I feel much better now. I'm going to get home before my husband sends out the cavalry to find me."

The crowd broke up one by one, leaving the room with murmurs of "take care," or "get some rest."

Humphreys was the last one remaining. "If you need to take tomorrow off to see a doctor, Mrs. Patterson, I completely understand. Besides, tomorrow is Friday, which means you'd have a three-day weekend to get some rest. Especially if you are…expecting."

"Oh no, I'm fine, Mr. Humphreys. Really, I am. I'll just swing by the drugstore on my way home and grab what I need. I'll be here in the morning."

"If you're sure?"

Sandy sent him a reassuring smile. "I am."

Chapter Ten

Sandy spent the next fifteen minutes in her classroom, talking with her friend Julia on the phone, voicing her fears about her possible pregnancy.

"I know I should be excited, but I'm not ready to be a mother, Julia. I'm only twenty-five years old, and my career has literally just begun. I've only been working for a week."

"What will you do?" Julia's quiet question sent Sandy's mind into a whirlwind.

"I don't know what I'm going to do. I just know that this can't be happening right now."

"Have you told Clark?"

Sandy rubbed at her forehead. "No. Clark doesn't know. I'm not even sure yet. But if I am pregnant, it couldn't have come at a worse time."

Of course, thinking about Clark's reaction to the possibility of being a father made Sandy inwardly smile. *Things will work out, and what's meant to be will be.*

The hair on the back of Sandy's neck suddenly stood up. She glanced up at her partially open door in time to see a shadow move away from the long, vertical window situated there.

She slowly stood and crept to the door. Carefully pulling it open, she poked her head out into the hall only to find it empty.

Mr. Cecil, the janitor, rounded a corner, push broom in hand.

Sandy asked Julia to hold on a second and then held the cell phone against her chest. "Hi, Mr. Cecil, did you happen to see someone in the hall just now?"

"No, ma'am. Is everything okay?"

Sandy glanced left and then right, but no one appeared in that hall but the janitor. Someone had been outside her door. Of that, she was certain. "Everything's fine, Mr. Cecil. I'll see you tomorrow."

Returning to her desk, Sandy said her goodbyes to Julia with a promise to call her later with her pregnancy test results. She then snatched up her purse and hurried from the building to her vehicle. She had a ten-minute drive ahead of her to the nearest drugstore.

To say that she was nervous would be an understatement. But a kernel of excitement rode beneath the surface. Though she was a little terrified of becoming a mother, she knew Clark would be ecstatic. Some of her anxiety settled.

Sandy arrived at the drugstore fifteen minutes later due to traffic being a nightmare. She switched off her car and got out, the cold winter wind whipping around her.

Thunder rolled in the distance, signaling the approach of a storm.

She hurried inside, zipping up her coat as she went.

"Welcome to Harden's Drugstore," the cashier in the front called out as Sandy made her way toward the feminine products aisle. "If I can help you find anything, let me know."

Sandy sent the woman a smile and a nod while keeping her focus on the task at hand.

She stopped in front of the pregnancy tests, unsure of which one to choose, finally settling on the more expensive one. Surely it would be the most accurate.

Making her way to the register, she set the test on the counter without meeting the gaze of the cashier.

After totaling up her purchase, the cashier placed the test in a bag while Sandy swiped her debit card. Sandy accepted her receipt and then lifted her gaze. "May I use your restroom?"

The cashier sent her a knowing smile. "Of course. It's in the back on the far left. You can't miss it."

Sandy thanked the woman, took her bag, and headed off in the direction of the restroom.

Once inside, she opened the box and took out one of the white test sticks. After reading the directions, she sat down to do what must be done.

Flushing the toilet, Sandy set the stick on the edge of the sink and washed her hands while preparing to wait.

She didn't have to wait long. A blue plus sign appeared within seconds, confirming what Sandy had already suspected. She was definitely pregnant.

Tears sprang to her eyes with the realization that she would soon be a mother.

All her fears suddenly seemed frivolous in the wake of what she now knew to be true. She couldn't wait to get home and tell Clark. The look on his face would be priceless.

Gathering up her test paraphernalia, Sandy put them back inside the bag and hurried out to her car.

She placed the bag along with her purse on the passenger seat and quickly left the drugstore. If she hurried, she would make it home before the storm hit.

Taking a left at the light, she decided to take the back roads to avoid the five o'clock traffic.

Though she didn't approve of texting and driving, Sandy dug out her cell phone with trembling hands and sent Clark a text. *Had to stop at the store. Be home soon.*

He didn't respond, which meant he was probably out feeding the cows, hoping to beat the rain.

Sandy glanced up at the black clouds gathering in the sky and pressed the gas pedal a little harder. If she didn't hurry, she would never make it home before the storm arrived.

A loud sound abruptly exploded from outside just seconds before her car jerked hard to the right.

Sandy's heart surged to her throat. She gripped the steering wheel with everything she had in an attempt to keep the car on the road. It took her a second to realize one of her tires had blown.

It took considerable effort to slow the vehicle and guide it off the edge of the road, but Sandy somehow managed it.

She sat there for long moments, attempting to slow her rapidly beating heart, and then opened her door and got out to assess the situation.

Her left front tire was shredded. But how was that possible? She'd just bought those tires not a month ago. She must have run over something.

Glancing up at the sky once more, Sandy exhaled a sigh and reached inside the car for her phone. She sent Clark another text. *Had a flat on Old Mill Rd. I'm okay. Will try to change it. Love you.*

Tossing her phone back onto the seat, Sandy popped the trunk, grabbed the spare along with the jack, and set about attempting to change the tire.

The sound of a vehicle pulling up behind her caught her attention.

She wiped the back of her hand across her forehead, squinting against the setting sun still peeking out from behind the gathering clouds in the sky.

Sandy pushed to her feet, brushed off her hands, and turned to face the person who'd stopped to help her.

Something slammed into the side of her head with enough force that Sandy flew against the side of her car. A bright light exploded behind her eyes, followed by white-hot agony. She opened her mouth to cry out, but no sound came forth.

Her world turned black.

Chapter Eleven

Sandy could only moan through the torturous throbbing taking place in her skull.

What had happened to her? Where was she? Had she been in an accident and was now in the hospital?

She remembered leaving the school and driving to the drugstore, recalled the thunder rolling through the sky.

"Clark?" she croaked, attempting to open her eyes, but something held them closed.

And then, memory returned with a vengeance. The pregnancy test, the flat tire... The blow to her head.

Her stomach lurched with the knowledge that someone had hit her.

She tried to lift her arms, but they were bound above her head. Her feet were secured to something as well.

"Help!" she attempted to scream, only to moan from the pain it caused.

Sandy tried forcing her eyes open once more, but quickly realized she'd been blindfolded.

Terror unlike any she'd ever known slid through her, locking her muscles and taking her breath. Someone had taken her.

She began to fight against her bonds, not caring about the pain her movements caused. She had to get free before—

"Shhhhh. Stop fighting," a voice whispered from somewhere above her. "Think about your condition."

Something about the voice sounded vaguely familiar to Sandy, but she couldn't place where she'd heard it. Not with the raspy whisper her captor used.

And what did they mean by "her condition?" Whoever it was obviously knew about her pregnancy. But how was that possible? She'd only just found out before her tire had blown. The only person who knew other than herself was Julia. And then, Sandy remembered the dizzy spell at the school.

Her mind tried to recall everyone in the room with her after she'd nearly fainted in the hall, but the memory was vague at best. She was fairly sure that Freedman, the grief counselor, Mr. Humphreys, and maybe Theresa were present in her classroom afterward. But the other faces were blank in Sandy's mind. "W-who are you? What do you want with me?"

Sandy strained to make out the person's features through the material of her blindfold, but she could see nothing other than an outline, and...long hair. Her captor was a woman?

"Heeeeelp," a hoarse-sounding voice pleaded from somewhere in another room.

Sandy's heartbeat accelerated once more. "Oh God, who is that? What's happening? Please let me go!" She began to yank on her bonds once again.

The woman standing over her reached down and gripped her chin in a tight hold. "You will calm down or I'll have to drug you. Understand?"

Forcing herself to still, Sandy concentrated on the whispery soft timbre of the woman's voice. "Why are you doing this?"

"Why do any of us do the things we do? Why is it that you thought to get rid of your unborn child when there are those in the world who would give anything to have one of their own?"

Sandy couldn't have heard the woman correctly. "W-what? I never planned on getting rid of my baby."

The reality of the situation was beginning to sink in. Sandy was being held against her will and would likely never make it out of there alive.

"Heeeeelp," the hoarse voice from the next room called out once more, only stronger this time.

Sandy recognized it as Reggie's. "Reggie!"

"Shut up," the woman standing over her rasped. "One more outburst from you and I'll kill him."

It took a second for Sandy to realize her blindfold was wet and another to understand she'd been crying. "Don't hurt him," she pleaded, straining to see through the now damp covering. "I'll do anything you want, just please don't hurt him."

A scratchy laugh echoed from above her. "You have no choice but to do what I want.

You're chained down in case you haven't noticed."

Sandy had noticed, all right. Her shoulders ached, and her wrists stung from yanking on her bonds.

Her mind turned to her unborn baby resting helplessly beneath her abdomen. With Sandy's arms and legs stretched out and restrained, her innocent child lay there exposed to whoever the monster was in the room. "P-please…"

But no answer came.

Sandy's head jerked from side to side, her hot, swollen eyes attempting to scan her surroundings from behind the cloth covering them. But all she could see was a light reflecting from above her.

And then the light suddenly went out, and the sound of a door closed to her left, telling her without words that the woman had left the room.

"Oh God…"

Chapter Twelve

Sandy had no idea how long she'd been lying there, chained down, when the need to relieve herself became excruciating.

She gritted her teeth and called out, "Helloooo?"

As much as she didn't want that terrifying woman back in the room with her, she would surely soil herself otherwise.

The sound of a door opening came from the left, and light could be seen through Sandy's blindfold. And then, the whisper-soft timbre of her captor's voice followed close behind it. "What is it?"

"I-I have to use the bathroom. I don't know how much longer I can hold it."

The feel of the buttons being opened on Sandy's shirt sent her into a full-on panic. She began to rear up, tossing her body from side to side. "No, no, no! What are you doing?"

Something sharp appeared at her throat. "Stop moving!" the woman hissed, her breath settling over Sandy's face like a musty blanket.

Sandy froze, her heart pounding so loudly in her ears she could hear nothing else.

The sharp object abruptly lifted, and the feel of her bra being severed between her breasts sent Sandy into another bout of panic. But she forced herself to remain still. She had no doubt the evil being hovering above her would cut her throat without a second thought.

The button on her pants was popped free next. Sandy fought down her terror, lying completely unmovable while her captor cut away her the remaining items she wore, including her underwear.

"Lift your bottom," the raspy voice demanded.

Sandy did as she was told, too afraid not to.

And then something cold appeared beneath her backside.

"It's a bedpan. Do your business and be quick about it."

Mortification warred with fear, but fear won out in the end.

Sandy squeezed her eyes tightly shut and allowed her bladder to empty itself.

Once she was done, the demented woman removed the bedpan and apparently set it on the floor, if the clanking sound were any indication.

"Get some sleep," the woman demanded in an eerily soft voice. "I'll be back soon."

Sandy listened to the sound of shoes slapping on the floor, and then a door closed, followed by total darkness once again.

She lay there, completely naked, spread out in a vulnerable position, unable to do anything but listen to the rapid beating of her own heart.

Another door opened in the distance, and Reggie's cries soon ricocheted off the walls of his own prison.

Sandy could hear him begging, pleading with the woman to kill him, to put him out of his misery.

He suddenly grew quiet, and the steady sounds of bedsprings bouncing inside a mattress began to fill Sandy's room.

It didn't take a genius to figure out what was happening to Reggie.

"Oh God," Sandy moaned, her stomach lurching. She rolled her head to the side and retched, heaving again and again. Yet no matter how much she vomited, nothing could block out the reality of Reggie's assault.

* * * *

Sandy wasn't sure how much time had elapsed before the sickening noises coming from Reggie's prison finally stopped.

She could hear him moaning through the wall that obviously separated them, a sound she would never forget as long as she lived. Which, if she didn't keep her wits about her, probably wouldn't be long.

The light came on and the door to her room reopened, illuminating the outline of the woman's body.

From what Sandy could see through her thin blindfold, the woman wore some kind of robe or dress, and her hair hung loose over her shoulders.

She moved deeper into the room, cursing under her breath. "You've puked on the bed."

"I-I'm sorry."

The shoes slapping against the floor once more told Sandy that her captor was leaving the room.

Relief was instant, but short-lived. The maniac returned a moment later, dragging someone with her. "Get over there and clean up that vomit."

Sandy could hear sniffling sounds as someone approached, and then the feel of a wet cloth gently swiped across her face.

The sniffling grew louder, and a terrified voice whispered, "Mrs. Patterson?"

The loud crack of a palm meeting flesh resounded throughout the room, a feminine cry following immediately after.

"Clean up the puke and keep your mouth shut," their captor demanded, impatience lining her voice.

Sandy once again found the voice familiar, but her mind was far too scrambled to place where she'd heard it before. "D-do I know you?"

The room grew quiet, and then Sandy's blindfold was abruptly ripped away.

She blinked several times, her eyes adjusting to the light in the room, and looked up at the maniac standing over her.

A brown leather mask covered the woman's features but didn't hide the glittering insanity of her eyes. She glared down at Sandy, her mouth visible through a vertical slit in the material covering her face. "No, but you will."

Chapter Thirteen

Sandy was too horrified to respond.

The woman stood over her, her hand wrapped in the hair of the missing high school student, Rhonda Shivers.

Sandy chanced a glance at the terrified girl, instantly wishing she hadn't.

Rhonda had no clothes on, and mascara streaked her eyes from her obvious crying. Her bottom lip had a split near the corner, with dried blood surrounding it, and bruises peppered her breasts.

"Why?" was all Sandy could muster, shifting her gaze back to their captor.

Jerking Rhonda's head back at an awkward angle, the woman yanked the young girl backward and shoved her around the foot of Sandy's bed. "Get over there."

Sandy swiveled her head in their direction, realizing that another bed rested against the far wall.

The woman quickly secured Rhonda to the twin bed in the same fashion she'd bound Sandy.

She then straightened, turned to face a horrified Sandy, and slowly lifted the dress over her head.

Sandy bit back a scream. Was she planning to hurt her now?

"Shut your eyes, Rhonda," Sandy whispered, her voice trembling uncontrollably. "No matter what you hear…" Her words trailed off when the woman's dress whispered to the floor.

Against her will, Sandy's gaze lowered to a horrifically disfigured scar covering the majority of the woman's abdomen. "Please don't do this."

Without responding, the disfigured woman left the room.

"Rhonda?" Sandy whispered, twisting her head in the crying teen's direction. "I need you to listen to me."

Though the girl continued to cry, she met Sandy's gaze.

"I want you to stay as quiet as you can, do you understand? Don't anger her—it—whatever she is. Just do as she says and be as meek as possible."

"S-she's going to hurt me again," Rhonda burst out, growing more hysterical by the second.

Sandy attempted to soothe her. "Shhhhh. Not if you stay quiet and do as she says."

"Y-you don't know what she's capable of. She'll torture me!"

Sandy knew exactly what that monster was capable of. She'd heard her hurting Reggie not long ago.

"Listen to me, Rhonda. There's another person in the room next to us. There could be more than one, I don't know. But we're alive, and we're going to stay that way until help arrives."

Rhonda hiccupped. "No one knows where we are. Help is never going to arrive!"

Sandy could see Rhonda's hysteria mounting. "Shhhhh, help will arrive. My husband will have realized that I'm missing by now. He'll find us, Rhonda. You just have to hold on."

Sandy wasn't sure she believed her own words, but it was all she had at the moment.

Rhonda's eyes suddenly grew huge, and all the color drained from her face. "Noooooo!" she began to scream, her arms and legs jerking against her bonds.

Sandy's head snapped in the direction of Rhonda's gaze to see the masked woman reentering the room, holding a knife in one hand and what could only be described as a black baton in her other. It resembled something a police officer would carry.

"Please don't do this," Sandy pleaded, watching the woman skirt her bed and head toward Rhonda. "I'm begging you! She's just an innocent young girl!"

The woman ignored Sandy's pleas, continuing on to the teenager's side.

Rhonda became hysterical, her screams exploding throughout the room to echo off the walls of their prison.

"Hey!" Sandy snarled, yanking on her bonds, her fear lending a false sense of courage that could possibly get her killed. "Leave her alone, you monster!"

"Monster?" the woman repeated in a deadly soft tone. She met Sandy's gaze from behind the eyeholes of that leather mask. "You haven't seen a monster… Yet."

Without taking her gaze from Sandy, she guided that baton to the juncture of Rhonda's thighs and thrust upward.

Rhonda's tormented screams filled the room, swirling around inside Sandy's head in a horrific cry of agony that ripped her heart in half.

Sandy squeezed her eyes shut to block out the sight, but nothing could shut out the agonizing sounds. They grew in volume, with every torturous thrust of that baton.

Seconds, minutes, hours passed. Sandy wasn't sure how long Rhonda's assault lasted when her screams eventually turned to exhausted moans.

But Sandy kept her eyes shut, too afraid of what she would find if she opened them.

"You will watch," the woman announced in a singsong voice, the sound almost as terrifying as Rhonda's screams.

Strong fingers suddenly gripped Sandy's face, and something sharp pressed just beneath her right eye. "Open them."

A pleading sound escaped Sandy's throat. She forced her eyes open, praying to God the manic woman didn't bury a knife in one of them.

Those insane eyes glittered back at her from behind that mask. "You will watch. If you close your eyes again, I will cut her throat."

Releasing Sandy's face, the naked woman moved back to Rhonda's side and continued the horrific violation of the young girl's body.

Sandy forced her horror-filled gaze to Rhonda's face. The agony registered there was a living, breathing thing that destroyed something in Sandy's soul. No matter what the outcome of their imprisonment, Sandy knew that Rhonda would be forever changed.

And then, the young girl rolled her head in Sandy's direction, revealing the true extent of her nightmare. Her eyes pleaded for Sandy to help her, to do something—anything to end her pain.

Sandy lifted her gaze to the masked maniac wielding that baton. "Take me instead…"

Chapter Fourteen

Terrified beyond words, Sandy watched the woman remove that baton from Rhonda Shivers' body and slowly head in her direction.

She ran the tip of the now bloody baton down Sandy's naked chest, stopping when she reached her stomach.

She dragged the weapon along Sandy's abdomen. "You would like that, wouldn't you? To harm the baby you carry."

Sandy swallowed back her bile, nearly choking on her next words. "W-why are you doing this?"

The baton suddenly stilled. "It's selfish women like you who produce monsters like me. You, with your Mayberry farm, doting husband, and parents who gave you everything. Yet you're too self-centered to appreciate what you have."

Confused by the woman's words, Sandy tried to keep her talking. Anything to prevent her from using that baton. "I-I know I'm fortunate. I—"

"Shut up!" the woman sneered, pressing that baton painfully against Sandy's abdomen. "I know what you planned to do."

Sandy shook her head, tears spilling from her eyes. "I don't understand what you want from me."

The feel of that baton sliding lower shot terror up Sandy's spine. "Please, just tell me what I've done, why I'm here. I've never hurt anyone in my life. I—"

"Yet you would harm an innocent baby," the woman interrupted, pressing the baton forward. "Your own child. Your flesh and blood. Now, who's the real monster here?" She pressed the baton forward.

Sandy went wild. Using all her strength, she flailed her body from side to side, attempting to dislodge that baton.

The sound of a doorbell echoed in the distance. The woman froze, then removed the baton and jumped to her feet.

Someone was at the door.

Hope flared to life inside Sandy. She opened her mouth to scream for help but was cut short by a sudden blow to the side of her head.

* * * *

Sandy's eyes fluttered open to darkness. She stared up in confusion, her brain strangely disconnected.

She moved to turn onto her side. But the pain screaming in her shoulder stopped her.

Colder than she'd ever been in her life, she quickly sat up, only to notice she wasn't in her bed. And she wore no clothes.

Memory came rushing back, and with it, bone-chilling panic. She'd been abducted and held prisoner by a maniac wearing a leather mask. The woman had chained her to a bed, and...

"Rhonda?" Sandy frantically whispered, realizing her arms and legs were no longer bound.

She threw her feet over the side of the bed and stood.

With her arms out in front of her, Sandy made her way in the direction where Rhonda was chained.

Her knees suddenly bumped into the side of the mattress.

"Rhonda?" she whispered again, her trembling hands coming into contact with Rhonda's ice-cold body.

Something sticky and wet coated the side of Rhonda's chest and neck, and the metallic smell of blood invaded Sandy's nostrils.

"No. Oh God, no! Rhonda?" Frantically feeling around the teenager's body, it didn't take Sandy long to realize the girl was dead. Rigor mortis had already set in. Which meant Rhonda had been dead for at least three to four hours.

Sandy dropped to her knees next to Rhonda's bed, her tears falling uncontrollably. Though it was too dark to see in their small prison, Sandy knew that Rhonda's throat had been cut. She'd felt the enormous amount of blood on her neck.

How long had that monster tortured Rhonda before taking her life?

More tears leaked from Sandy's eyes.

Another thought occurred to her. Why had the woman removed Sandy's chains? Was she in the room with her now, waiting to kill her too?

Unable to control her fear, Sandy pushed unsteadily to her feet. With her arms out in front of her, she moved slowly in the direction she remembered the door being.

Her legs trembled so much, they nearly buckled on her a few times before she reached the door.

Gripping the knob in both hands, Sandy twisted it with every ounce of strength she had, only to realize it was locked.

She pulled, yanked, and slammed into the heavy wood, but it wouldn't budge. "Pleaseeeee," she cried, laying her face against the freezing cold surface of that door.

No one came.

Chapter Fifteen

Sandy spent what seemed hours moving around her prison, feeling along the walls in search of a way out, only to end up where she'd started... At the door. She flipped the light switch again and again, but the room remained dark.

The woman must have turned off the breaker since there had been a light previously on in that room.

Sandy had gone beyond cold, to the point that her toes hurt, as did her back. It had to be at least thirty degrees in her small prison, and she had no clothing or blankets to cover herself with.

Her mind drifted back to Rhonda Shivers and the torture she'd endured at the hands of that monster. Rhonda had been only sixteen years old, a beautiful girl with a bright future ahead of her. And she'd been killed unmercifully.

Sandy felt the familiar sting, the burning sensation behind her eyes, yet the tears refused to come. She'd cried so much for so long, her eyes were nearly swollen shut. She didn't need light to figure that out; she could feel them throbbing in their sockets.

My baby, came her next thought, her palm moving to cover her unborn child. If she didn't find a way to get out of there, and quick, her baby would never survive.

A light suddenly appeared beneath the door, allowing Sandy to partially see.

She scrambled back to her bed, laid on her back, and quickly closed her eyes.

The sound of footsteps moving in her direction sent Sandy's stomach tightening in dread. The psychopath had returned.

Forcing herself to relax as much as her freezing body would allow, Sandy slowed her breathing. If she appeared to be unconscious, maybe the sadistic fiend would leave without hurting her.

The door opened, and the side of Sandy's bed dipped with someone's weight.

Sandy held completely still, when every muscle in her body was poised for flight.

And then, the feel of fingers touching her mouth nearly did her in. Sandy willed the nausea threatening to calm by pushing the image of that maniac from her mind.

Breathe, Sandy silently repeated again and again. *Just breathe.*

Hot, stale breath washed over Sandy's face, and then a mouth settled over her lips.

Sandy wanted to lash out, to puke, to scream, to run from that place and never look back. But she couldn't. Something inside her warned her to remain still, or she'd end up like poor Rhonda Shivers on the next bed, lying in a pool of her own blood.

Sandy knew in that moment that she would do anything to stay alive, to save her unborn child, no matter what she had to do to make that happen.

She allowed her lips to slightly part.

A hand slipped behind Sandy's neck, and the mouth resting over hers began to move, applying enough pressure to open Sandy's mouth further.

She didn't resist or fight; she simply lay there, unmoving, pliant and submissive.

The lips lifted, saving Sandy from vomiting. They drifted down her body to be joined by a pair of roaming hands.

No, God, please no, Sandy silently pleaded, praying that the sick, sadistic monster didn't do what she knew she was about to do.

But the mouth stopped at Sandy's abdomen, and the woman's leather-covered face began to nuzzle the skin there.

Sandy cracked her eyes open enough to see the masked woman leaning over her unborn child.

And then, one word slipped from the psycho's lips. "Mine."

Sandy's heart jackknifed. Had that maniac been referring to her or her unborn baby? Sandy fought a shudder.

The hands and mouth were suddenly gone. The sound of the door closing and locking could be heard a moment later.

Sandy sat up in bed, her eyes attempting to adjust to the darkness to no avail. The light in the hall had been extinguished, casting Sandy's prison into an inky blackness once more.

She strained to hear, wondering if the woman had left, or if she planned on returning to torture her.

Another door slammed shut on the other side of the wall, and Reggie's horrific moans began anew.

Sandy fell back on the bed, covering her ears with her hands. But nothing could block out the hoarse screams of Reggie's cries, nor the disgusting sounds of those mattress springs that soon followed after.

Sandy began to hum deep in her throat, the vibration of her voice drowning out some of the horror going on in the next room. But it didn't slow her thoughts or the nightmarish images of Reggie plaguing her terrified mind…

Chapter Sixteen

Sandy's shivering eventually forced her to remove her palms from her ears. She huddled in the fetal position, placing her hands between her knees for warmth.

The silence surrounding her became deafening the longer she lay there, listening for signs of life coming from Reggie's room. But it had grown quiet long ago.

A light abruptly came on in the hallway, and the door was thrown open.

"I see you're awake," the masked woman announced, stepping into the room. She held a tray in one hand and a blanket in the other.

Flipping on the light, she barked, "Sit up."

Sandy squinted against the brightness. She wanted to ask the woman about Reggie, but she didn't dare. If the psycho didn't torture him again, she would likely hurt Sandy for questioning her.

Sandy sat up and met the woman's masked gaze. "How long have I been here?"

"Two days," the woman answered in a matter-of-fact tone.

Clark has to be frantic by now. Swallowing around a parched throat, Sandy watched the woman move in her direction, holding that tray. She also noticed a knife clutched tightly in one of her hands.

"Take the blanket and the tray."

Sandy did as she was told, quickly wrapping the blanket around her chilled form and then accepting the tray.

"Now eat."

How was she supposed to eat with poor Rhonda Shivers' dead body lying not five feet to her left? But she had no choice if she expected to stay alive. Especially since she carried another life inside her.

Sandy peered down at the tray, noticing eggs, bacon, and toast resting on a plate. A glass of orange juice sat next to it.

She picked up the juice and drank deeply before snatching up the bacon and eating like a woman starved. She didn't dare glance over at Rhonda.

Realizing there were no utensils, Sandy whispered without looking up, "How am I going to eat the eggs?"

"With your fingers, you spoiled, self-centered excuse for a human."

Sandy flinched from the venomous sound of the woman's voice and continued to eat with her head lowered.

She could see the woman moving in her peripheral, stopping next to the bed Rhonda lay on.

The chains began to clink together, telling Sandy without words that Rhonda's body was being released.

Sandy chanced a glance in their direction, nearly choking on her food when Rhonda's head came into view. Blood. So much dried blood.

Nausea was instant.

Unable to bear the sight, Sandy squeezed her eyes shut, listening as the psycho dropped Rhonda's body to the floor and dragged her from the room.

Once the door closed behind them, Sandy shoved her tray off her lap, rolled to the side, and vomited into her bedpan.

She stayed in that position for long moments, moaning, unable to get Rhonda's image from her mind.

Her psychotic captor was obviously getting ready to dump Rhonda somewhere in the woods, just as she'd done with the others. And Sandy had no doubt that the woman who'd taken her, Rhonda, and Reggie was the same person who'd killed all the others.

Another thought occurred to her as she remained there with her head hanging over the side of the bed. The police were searching for a man responsible for the murders. They would never think to look for a woman.

Sandy shuddered with the last heave and pushed weakly back into a sitting position. She set the tray of food onto the floor and then returned to the fetal position to huddle deep inside the blanket.

Was this it for her? Did that demented psycho plan to kill her next, or would she simply toy with Sandy until she grew tired of her? Why had she fed Sandy and offered her a blanket? Sandy didn't know, but if she had any hopes of staying alive, she needed to figure it out and quick.

Long minutes passed without incident before the light disappeared, casting the room in total darkness. The woman must have flipped the breaker again.

Sandy remained on her side, straining to hear something—anything that would help her out of her situation—but she was met with silence.

No television played nearby, no radio or footsteps in the distance. No doors opened and closed, nor did Sandy hear any kitchen appliances in use.

How did one live and function in a house without making a sound? Unless...Sandy was being held in a basement of sorts. But what about Reggie? She knew he was somewhere on the other side of the wall.

Nothing made sense.

And then something Clark had told her before tickled at the edges of her mind. She concentrated on his handsome face, recalling a conversation they'd had shortly before their wedding.

"I saw on the news today that they found the body of Maryann Jones," Sandy announced when Clark entered the house. "She'd been sexually assaulted, beaten beyond recognition, and starved to death. What kind of a man would do such a thing to another person?"

Clark shook his head and hung his hat on a hook by the door. "A monster, that's who."

Trailing across the room, Clark wrapped his wife in a hug. "Don't waste your energy trying to understand the mind of a psychopath. They don't think the way we do. You're trying to put logic with illogic. It won't work."

"Logic with illogic," Sandy whispered aloud, her mind floating back to the present.

She shifted to her other side, staring into the darkness, her thoughts scattered in every direction imaginable. How did one think illogically?

Sandy slowed her breathing as much as her body would allow in its current condition. Fear had her muscles tight, her mind racing. If she had any hope of getting out of there alive, she would need to get it together and think.

Think like a killer…

Chapter Seventeen

Sandy's captor returned twice that day. Once to empty her bedpan and once to bring her more food. She didn't speak or answer any of Sandy's nervously spoken questions.

But hours of being left alone in the darkness had given Sandy time to think. As sickening as it was to conjure up images of Rhonda Shivers, that's exactly what she did.

Rhonda had been assaulted with that baton, beaten, and then suffered her throat being cut. What was it about Rhonda that enraged the woman to the point of torturing her?

Sandy then thought about Maryann Jones, the seventeen-year-old whose body was found a year earlier. She'd experienced the same death as Rhonda had. Yet, the killer had kept Maryann for a month before disposing of her in a place where she was sure to be found.

Destiny Murray had also been a victim of the same killer, her body discovered less than five miles from her home. She had been beaten, raped, and tortured.

Destiny Murray, the first girl to go missing more than two years ago. Same cause of death. And she'd been dumped less than ten miles from her home.

Heidi Birch had been missing for just over a month before her body was discovered. As with the others, she had been killed in the same fashion and discarded in a nearby wooded area.

In her mind, Sandy went over every detail that she could remember about each case, hoping to piece together the killer's motives for choosing those particular girls.

Okay. They all attended the same school, Purvis High. What else did they have in common?

Sandy closed her eyes, her mind crawling over everything she'd read or watched on television about the murders.

All the victims had long dark hair and possibly green eyes. She wasn't a hundred percent sure about the eye color of each one, but she didn't recall a mention of brown or blue.

The girls probably didn't run in the same circles, since some were seniors and some juniors. In fact, Sandy was pretty sure one had been a sophomore.

According to the news reports, Maryann Jones had been a straight A student and captain of the volleyball team. She'd never been in trouble as far as Sandy knew and had come from a good home.

Destiny Murray had been a cheerleader, made good grades as well, and like Maryann, had come from a good home.

Sandy slowly sat up, pieces of the puzzle connecting in her mind. All the girls had been exceptional students. Each one had come from a good home, and they were all very active in school.

There's the connection. But why take them, torture them, and kill them? And why take me? I don't fit that bill.

But Sandy had graduated from Purvis High School eight years earlier. She had made good grades, and she had come from a great home.

She also realized she had the same hair and possibly the same eye color as the other girls.

It still made no sense. Unless the killer worked at Purvis High School.

Sandy suddenly recalled something the woman had said to her. *"Why do any of us do the things we do? Why is it that you thought to get rid of your unborn child when there are those in the world who would give anything to have one of their own?"*

Another memory skated through Sandy's mind. *"It's selfish women like you who produce monsters like me. You, with your Mayberry farm, doting husband, and parents who gave you everything. Yet you're too self-centered to appreciate what you have."*

More of the woman's words tickled at Sandy's psyche. *"Yet you would harm an innocent baby. Your own child. Your flesh and blood. Now, who's the real monster here?"*

Sandy had never intended to harm her child. Sure, she'd been afraid and upset by the prospect of being pregnant at twenty-five, but she would have never done anything to hurt her baby.

The strangest thing of all was that no one knew of Sandy's pregnancy but Julia and the small gathering in the school hall when Sandy had nearly fainted.

Realization suddenly dawned. The killer, the woman who'd abducted her and those girls, worked at Purvis High School. But who was she?

Theresa Little, the PE coach had been in the hall the day Sandy had nearly fainted. So had Mrs. Tate, the grief counselor. Earlene Freedman had been present as well, and Sandy was pretty certain she remembered the English teacher, Miss Baker, being there.

There were a couple more women in the hall that day, yet Sandy couldn't recall who. The only others who'd been present before she'd left the school were Mr. Humphreys and Mr. Cecil, the janitor.

Something else came to her the longer she sat there, searching her memories. The shadow outside her classroom door while she'd been on the phone with Julia. Someone had been out there, listening. And not just someone, but the woman who'd hit Sandy in the head and brought her to the Hell she now found herself in.

Theresa Little came to mind. She had the strength to carry out an abduction. Yet Theresa had blonde hair. The woman wearing the mask was a brunette. *Unless it's a wig…*

Earlene Freedman's words flashed through Sandy's mind. *"You're not pregnant, are you?"*

Mrs. Freedman definitely had long dark hair, and Sandy had thought the teacher's attitude about the missing girls had been uncalled for. Especially when Freedman announced, *"Hopefully, it'll be a lesson to these irresponsible teenagers. If they'd just adhere to the curfew set up for their protection and have their butts at home when they're supposed to, none of this would be happening."*

Though Sandy knew that Freedman had spoken the truth, she couldn't wrap her mind around *how* Freedman spoke it. Her words had fairly dripped with condemnation.

And then there was the introvert, Marcy Baker, who'd sat in that teacher's lounge, shifty eyed and wearing that floral print dress. A forty-year-old woman never married and no social skills to speak of.

The list went on in Sandy's mind until she could barely hold her eyes open another minute. She was beyond exhausted, to the point of delirium.

Just before she drifted off, her mind conjured up the grief counselor, Mrs. Tate, a woman who counseled the grieving, who had access to those girls' innermost thoughts and feelings. A woman with a possible motive...

Chapter Eighteen

Sandy jerked awake at the sound of sobbing somewhere nearby.

The light was suddenly turned on in her room and the door thrown open.

A gasp of denial burst forth when Mindy Reyes was shoved into the room.

Mindy's gaze immediately locked on Sandy, revealing the horror and disbelief warring inside her.

"Over there," the mask-wearing psycho demanded, gripping a knife in one hand and giving Mindy a push with the other.

Sandy's stomach knotted up in terror. She had to do something and fast before that maniac hurt the Reyes girl.

Rolling to her side, Sandy pulled her knees up to her chest and moaned deep in her throat.

The woman glanced in Sandy's direction, but the mask she wore hid her expression. "What's wrong with you?"

"My stomach," Sandy groaned, hoping her face conveyed pain.

Chaining Mindy to the bed, the masked woman moved to Sandy's side. "What about your stomach?"

"It hurts..."

The woman stood there, staring down at her for so long Sandy thought for sure she'd seen through her attempted deception.

And then she spoke. "Get up."

Sandy carefully eased her feet over the side of the bed, still hunched over and clutching her abdomen.

The woman touched her on the neck with the knife she held. "Walk slowly. One wrong move on your part, and I won't hesitate to kill you."

For some reason, Sandy wasn't sure the woman would actually kill her, but she wasn't willing to take that chance. Besides, she couldn't risk the woman hurting Mindy.

Still hunched over, Sandy moved toward the door.

"Go left," the woman demanded from somewhere close behind her.

Once in the hall, Sandy got a good look at her surroundings. She was in a large basement of sorts, just as she'd suspected.

A hand pressed against her back. "Up the stairs."

Sandy feigned another moan while making her way to the steep stairs, her eyes darting from corner to corner of that basement.

Another room sat off to her left, the door closed, and no light seeping out from under it. That had to be where Reggie was being kept.

Lifting her foot to the bottom step, Sandy forced another painful sound and then began her ascent up the stairs.

"Open the door," came the impatient growl from behind her.

Sandy stopped at the top of the stairs and gripped the knob. With a twist of her hand, she opened the door and pushed it wide.

A brightly lit kitchen came into view, neat and clean and boasting of stainless-steel appliances.

More than a little surprised by the normalcy of it, Sandy could only stare. What did she expect, cobwebs and blood?

"Move!" the woman barked, jerking Sandy out of her shocked state. "In that room up ahead to your left."

Sandy fought the urge to run. But the psychotic woman would be on her before she could make it out of that kitchen. Sandy had seen the knife the woman held and had no doubts that she'd bury it in Sandy's back before she could find an exit.

Stopping in front of the door the woman had indicated, Sandy opened it and stepped inside.

A full-size four-poster bed sat in the center, with a nightstand on either side. Chains hung from the posts, leaving little doubt as to what the woman had in mind.

Sandy's gaze darted to the single window in the room, only to find it covered in bars.

Another door sat off to the right of the bed, leaving Sandy to wonder if it led to a bathroom.

She didn't have long to wonder.

"Get in the bathroom," the masked woman rasped, once more giving Sandy a shove.

Sandy stumbled forward past the bed and into the bathroom.

The woman flipped on the light and pointed to the shower. "I want you to bathe. Once you're finished, you will get in that bed and keep your mouth closed. If you make a sound, the Reyes girl will suffer for it. Do I make myself clear?"

Sandy nodded, turned on the water, and stepped under the warm spray.

It didn't surprise her that the woman knew Mindy's name. Sandy had already surmised that the monster worked at the high school.

Glancing to her right, she briefly locked gazes with the eyes staring back at her from the holes in that leather mask. The psycho looking back at her planned on watching her bathe.

"Hurry it up," Leather Face demanded, sending Sandy scrambling for the shampoo resting on a shelf in the shower.

She quickly washed her hair and then her body before turning off the shower and stepping out.

The woman nodded toward a towel hanging from a rack. "Dry off and make it quick."

Sandy did as she was told, all the while keeping up the appearance of being in pain. "Do you have a name?"

That gave the psycho pause.

"I-it doesn't have to be your real name. Just —"

"Joan," the woman rasped, cutting off the rest of Sandy's words. "You may call me Joan."

Chapter Nineteen

Sandy's heart pounded in fear, shock, and disbelief. The mask-wearing serial killer had just referred to herself as Joan.

Though Sandy doubted it was her real name, it somehow humanized her in Sandy's eyes. "Thank you for telling me your name."

And then, another thought occurred to her. Joan could very well be the woman's real name, and if so, she felt secure enough to tell Sandy because she knew Sandy would never make it out of there alive.

Sandy swallowed around a throat gone dry.

"Move to the bed," Joan demanded, jerking her chin in the direction of the open doorway.

Sandy bit the inside of her lips to keep her tears at bay and did as Joan ordered.

Stopping at the side of the bed, Sandy took in the chains, knowing full well what would happen next.

"Up!"

Sandy scrambled forward, grateful for the covers the bed would provide.

Joan yanked them away. "Lie on your back and spread your arms and legs."

"Please," Sandy whispered, the tears forming against her will. "Please don't chain me. I won't fight, I swear it."

The knife was at her throat in an instant, that leather mask inches from Sandy's face. "Do as you are told."

Too afraid to do anything else, Sandy laid back and spread her limbs, both mortified and terrified at the same time.

Joan went about chaining her wrists and ankles to the bedposts.

Obviously satisfied that Sandy was secure, Joan placed the knife on the nightstand and crawled up on the bed next to her.

Nausea reared its head again. Sandy could feel the tears tracking down the sides of her face to disappear into her hairline. Her throat had closed up to the point where she found it hard to swallow, to breathe.

Joan opened the drawer on the nightstand and withdrew something.

Too terrified to look, Sandy stared up at the ceiling through the tears swimming in her eyes.

"Lift your head," Joan rasped, that hideous mask appearing in Sandy's peripheral.

Raising her head off the pillow, Sandy moaned in terror as the woman covered her eyes like she'd done before, blindfolding her and throwing the room into darkness.

A rustling sound reached Sandy's ears, and she realized that Joan had removed her mask.

"I'm going to check you now. If you fight me or tense up in the least, I *will* hurt the Reyes girl. Do you understand?"

A soft cry of defeat escaped Sandy. How was she expected not to tense up when she had no idea what this fiend was about to do to her?

"Okay then." Joan moved to get up.

"I understand," Sandy cried, her head turning in the direction of her captor. "I won't fight, just please don't hurt her."

The feel of that evil psycho slithering down the bed sent Sandy's skin crawling, but nothing felt as demeaning as the woman's weight settling between her open legs.

Sandy attempted to block her out, to think about something — anything but what she knew was about to happen. She envisioned Clark, the night he proposed to her. The smile on his face on their wedding day. The morning he'd slipped on the ice in the yard, and the two of them laughed until their sides hurt.

She thought about the look of pride in his eyes the day she'd graduated from college. The love he'd always shown her, the lifelong friendship he represented. *I love you, Clark. I will always love you.*

The feel of the woman's fingers entering her body yanked Sandy out of her thoughts of Clark, quickly producing more tears of denial.

Then, a hand flattened above her pubic bone, pushing downward while the fingers inside her pressed almost painfully upward.

Though Sandy gasped from the invasion, she held completely still, afraid the next invasion she suffered would be from the blade of the knife Joan held.

The fingers suddenly disappeared as did the palm against her abdomen. "There is no bleeding. You will stay in this room at night.

During the day, you will be moved back below."

Sandy thought that an odd thing to say. Why would the woman need to move her to the basement during the day, unless she had to work? And Sandy was almost a hundred percent certain the woman known as Joan worked at the school.

No, Joan couldn't risk leaving Sandy in a room with the possibility that someone outside would hear her screams.

The feel of the bed moving brought Sandy out of her thoughts and back to her tormented reality.

Joan's weight suddenly settled over her, pressing Sandy's body deeper into the mattress.

She rested her cheek against the side of Sandy's face and breathed into her ear. "Do you know how fortunate you are to carry that life inside you?"

Sandy's entire body trembled in fear and disgust. "Y-yes."

Long moments passed in silence. And then, "Do you know what I want you to do, Sandy?"

Afraid to ask, yet more afraid not to, Sandy whispered through her tears, "W-what?"

"Kiss me."

By now, Sandy was in full-on gag mode, her stomach on the verge of projectile vomiting. But then, Joan's next words sealed her fate. "If you don't think you can handle that, I'm sure the little Reyes girl would be more than happy to."

Shutting down her emotions, Sandy slowly turned her face toward Joan's. No matter what she had to go through at the hands of that monster, she would do it to protect Mindy Reyes.

The sickening feel of the woman's lips sliding over her own brought forth a moan of disgust Sandy couldn't contain.

That didn't deter Joan in the least. She lifted her mouth enough to speak. "Tell me you love me."

More tears gushed from Sandy's eyes, soaking the blindfold covering her closed lids. She could feel her jaw trembling and knew her teeth would chatter if she opened her mouth.

"Tell me," Joan demanded, her disgusting breath bathing Sandy's face.

"I-I love you." Though Sandy managed to get the words out, they were barely a whisper.

"Again..."

So much hatred and disgust swam inside Sandy's mind in that moment. If she ever did manage to get free, she would take great pleasure in killing the woman named Joan. No matter how she had to do it. "I love you."

Chapter Twenty

Sandy rolled to her side the second Joan left the room.

The sadistic monster had molested her, had forced her to do things she had never imagined in her darkest nightmares. She'd then unchained all Sandy's limbs but her left wrist, covered her with a blanket, and removed her blindfold.

Of course, the mask had been put back on the psycho's face beforehand.

Sandy stared at the bar-covered window, silently begging God to deliver her out of the hands of that monster. How was she ever going to escape the clutches of this horrific nightmare she found herself in?

Her stomach heaved, but she swallowed it back. She could still smell the woman's scent on her, the sick, musty odor of the psycho who'd molested her.

Don't throw up, she chanted again and again, hanging her head off the side of the bed, her mind reliving every torturous detail of what had happened to her.

She picked up the sheet with her free hand and scrubbed at her face in an attempt to rid herself of the woman's smell.

"Tell me you love me." Sandy couldn't shake the sound of that whispered demand swirling through her mind. Saying those three words aloud had been nearly as hard as suffering the woman's violation of her body.

Why would a serial killer, a psychopath that murdered young girls, demand Sandy speak words of love?

If Sandy threw up now, she had no doubt that Joan would punish her for it. So, she took deep breaths, in hopes of forcing back the bile. But the woman's scent continued to invade her.

Tears surfaced again, and with them, thoughts of Clark. He had to be going crazy by now, especially after discovering her car on the side of the road. And she knew he'd found it as surely as she knew he wouldn't give up looking for her.

Another despairing thought entered her mind. How would Clark, the police, or even the FBI ever find her? They were searching for a man.

The door opened again to admit Joan. She wore the same floral print dress and leather mask as before.

Without glancing in Sandy's direction, she strolled over to the television and switched it on to the local news channel.

She then scurried to the bathroom, returning a minute later with a glass of water, which she set on the nightstand.

"I'll be back later with some food," Joan rasped, heading toward the door. "Remember what I said. No noise."

Sandy could only nod, her gaze taking in everything about Joan's appearance. The woman's dark hair still hung over her shoulders, neat and obviously freshly brushed.

The buttons on her floral print dress were askew as if she'd missed a buttonhole when donning the hideous thing. A streak of blood marked her arm, blood that didn't belong to Sandy. Had she hurt Mindy Reyes? "I-is Mindy okay?"

Joan stopped at the door, her back to Sandy, before slowly turning to face her. "You care about a girl you barely know and yet not your own child?"

Sandy swallowed her fear and forced her next words past her lips. "I love my baby more than anything."

"You lie!" Joan snarled, storming back into the room. She stopped next to the bed, the palm of her hand connecting with Sandy's cheek.

Pain exploded in Sandy's face, eliciting a cry from her that she was powerless to stop.

"I heard you," Joan continued in that low, scratchy voice, suddenly gripping Sandy's chin in a painful hold. "You're no different than the rest. Selfish, pitiful excuse for a mother."

Sandy stared up at Joan in fear and confusion, wanting to look away but too afraid to risk it.

Joan finally released her. "You disgust me." Without another word, she spun on her heel and left the room, pulling the door closed behind her.

Sandy blew out a shaky, relieved breath, half expecting that door to be thrown open once more.

When that didn't happen, she shifted her gaze to the television sitting on the dresser.

The same anchorwoman she'd seen on the news only days before was speaking in a monotone voice. "*The body of a young girl has been discovered in a wooded area this afternoon. The police have not released a name at this time, as the body has yet to be identified.*"

The woman continued to speak, informing the public of as many details as she legally could without mentioning Rhonda Shiver's name. And she knew it to be Rhonda as well as Sandy did.

An image of Sandy suddenly flashed across the screen, the anchorwoman pausing for dramatic effect. "*Sandy Patterson is a twelfth-grade math teacher at Purvis High School. Her car was discovered abandoned on Old Mill Road three days ago, her purse and cell phone still inside. If you have any information leading to the whereabouts of Sandy Patterson, we implore you to contact the Montgomery Police Department."*

A number appeared beneath Sandy's photo. *"Miss Patterson's husband is here with us this evening..."*

The anchorwoman continued to speak, but Sandy no longer listened. Her gaze was instantly glued to Clark's tormented face, as he was now seated in front of the cameras.

He cleared his throat, his eyes full of fear and pleading. *"My name is Clark Patterson. My wife, Sandy, is missing. She left work three days ago after texting me that she was on her way home. She never made it."*

Clark's gaze bored into the camera. *"I don't know who took my Sandy, but if you're listening, I'm begging you not to hurt her. Please let her come back to me. Please, she's all I have…"* A lone tear leaked from the corner of his eye.

An anguished sound rose up in Sandy's throat.

The camera panned out until Clark disappeared altogether, and a commercial quickly followed.

Sandy's eyes slid shut, her mind conjuring up the memory of her beloved's face. She replayed every expression, every sorrowful word he'd spoken, until the cry trapped in her throat released to echo off the walls of her prison. *Clark…*

Chapter Twenty-One

Sandy spent the rest of the night in that room, her wrist chained to the bed.

Joan came in twice during that time to take Sandy to the bathroom.

She'd left the television on for Sandy to watch, which puzzled Sandy as much as it relieved her. The silence could be a torture all on its own.

Early the following morning, Sandy lay awake, watching the sun come up through her one window. She had now been missing for four days.

Joan entered the room, wearing that hideous mask and a dark-red robe. She held a knife in her hand and a key in the other.

Without speaking, she rounded the bed, pressed the blade of that knife to Sandy's throat, and leaned in close.

This is it, Sandy thought, too terrified to scream. She's going to kill me just as she did the others.

But Joan didn't kill her. She peered down at Sandy from the uneven holes in that mask and then lowered her face until her lips slanted across Sandy's.

The leather of that mask dragged across Sandy's top lip with every movement of Joan's disgusting mouth over hers.

Without warning, Joan lifted her head, paused for a moment, and then moved down Sandy's body to begin kissing her abdomen.

Sandy shrank back as far as the mattress would allow. Try as she might, she couldn't seem to force her body to relax.

"Mine," Joan whispered once more, giving Sandy's abdomen one last kiss.

Joan straightened, moved to Sandy's bound wrist, and released it. "Get up."

Sandy scrambled from the bed and staggered toward the door on rubbery legs. "Where are you taking me?"

A sharp sting near her left shoulder told Sandy without words that Joan had cut her.

Sandy cried out, hurrying forward to prevent the maniac from injuring her more.

"Keep your mouth shut," Joan hissed, tight on her heels. "Or the next one will be your throat."

Sandy staggered into the hall toward the kitchen, not needing to be told to head to the basement. It was rapidly becoming daylight, which meant that Joan would go to work and leave Sandy chained in the dark to await her return.

In that moment, it dawned on Sandy that Joan wanted her completely dependent. To remain naked and helpless until she decided otherwise.

They reached the basement, and Sandy moved to the room she'd previously been held in.

She opened the door without being told, surprised to find the light on inside.

Mindy Reyes lay on her back, chained to the cot Rhonda had been bound to. Her legs and arms were full of long dark bruises from what Sandy assumed came from the baton. Blood was smeared on her thighs as well as her face.

She moaned deep in her throat, her head turning in Sandy's direction. The look in her eyes could only be described as terror.

"You said you wouldn't hurt her," Sandy whispered, unable to stop the tears from tracking down her face. "Y-you said if I did what you wanted that you wouldn't touch her."

Joan stormed forward, backhanding Sandy onto her own twin bed. "You dare to question me? Nothing you've done has pleased me, you ungrateful hypocrite. You are alive because of me, and you would do well to remember that."

Sandy knew she'd screwed up. She had angered Joan to the point where the eyes looking at her from the holes of that mask were huge and unfocused.

Joan abruptly stormed from the room, slamming the door shut behind her.

Sandy was too afraid to move for fear she'd return and follow through with her threats.

The faint sound of Reggie's cries suddenly filled the room, slicing through Sandy's heart with a pain that staggered her. His voice was so weak, it could barely be heard through the wall that separated them.

And then the muffled squeaking of the bedsprings filled the air, drowning out the barely audible moans Reggie made.

"Oh God." Sandy wept, unable to block out the horror she knew Reggie experienced at the hands of the monster known as Joan.

What felt like hours passed before the sounds of those bedsprings suddenly stopped, leaving an eerie silence in their wake.

A door slammed a short time later, signaling Joan's departure from the basement.

Sandy held perfectly still, half expecting the psycho to appear in her room, but the basement remained quiet. And Joan had left the light on.

Chapter Twenty-Two

"Shhhhhh," Sandy shushed, terrified that Mindy's sobs would summon the Devil in that leather mask. "She'll hear you."

Mindy continued to cry. "Help me!"

"Listen to me," Sandy implored her, rushing to the girl's side. "If she hears you, she'll only come back to hurt you more. You have to stay quiet."

Sandy tried not to look at the condition of Mindy's battered body, but against her will, her gaze strayed down the length of the girl.

From the amount of blood pooling on that mattress, she had no doubt that Joan had assaulted Mindy with that baton, just as she had Rhonda. And Mindy was bleeding badly.

Panicked, Sandy searched the room for something—anything—to staunch the blood flow, but there was nothing there.

"Try not to move," Sandy whispered before rushing over to her own bed. She dropped to her knees, locked her teeth onto the mattress, and ripped a hole in the material. She then hooked her fingers inside and yanked with everything she had, tearing a long strip of the cloth free.

Hurrying back to Mindy's side, Sandy wadded up the material and pressed it between the girl's thighs. "This should help slow the bleeding. Hold as still as you can, okay? I'll see if I can get these chains off you."

Mindy looked up at her through her tears, a tiny spark of hope in her green eyes.

Sandy quickly straightened, her fingers going to the chained cuffs surrounding Mindy's wrists. The cuffs were so tight, there would be no way she could remove Mindy's hands from their hold.

She checked the young girl's feet next, only to find her ankles chained as tightly as her wrists. "I — they're — I can't get them off. They're on there too tight."

"Pleaseeeee," Mindy wailed. She began struggling anew.

Sandy quickly grabbed at Mindy's arms in an attempt to prevent her from damaging herself further.

"You have to stop, Mindy! I can't help you if you don't stop fighting."

Something in Sandy's voice must have reached the girl's terrified mind. She slowed her movements, but the tears continued to fall.

Releasing her hold on Mindy's arms, Sandy straightened and ran a hand down her face.

A thought occurred to her. She ran over to the wall, pressed her forehead against it, and called out, "Reggie? Reggie, can you hear me?"

Silence.

She tried again, louder this time. "Reggie! It's Mrs. Patterson!"

No sounds could be heard on the other side of that wall.

Disappointed beyond words, Sandy spun around and ran to the door, but of course, it was locked.

She slowly turned back to face a devastated Mindy, whose crying once more grew in volume. Yet, Sandy knew there would be nothing she could do to calm her. Mindy knew there was no way out as well as Sandy did.

Sandy moved on wooden legs back to her bed, attempting to block out the heart-wrenching cries coming from Mindy Reyes, to no avail. The sounds embedded themselves deep into Sandy's psyche, where she knew they would remain until she drew her last breath.

* * * *

Sandy had shivered for so long, her entire body hurt from it. She knew Mindy was just as cold; she'd been listening to her teeth chatter for hours.

Mindy's bleeding had stopped long ago, as had her cries. For which Sandy was grateful. She hadn't been able to think past the tormented sound.

With the room in some semblance of silence, a plan had begun to form.

Sandy had thought about everything she'd seen and heard since her abduction. Her mind had gone over every detail of Joan, no matter how small it might seem. Joan definitely worked at Purvis High School, as well as being present in the hall the day Sandy had nearly fainted. Which narrowed things down to a small handful of people.

Other details Sandy had noted were that Joan hadn't hurt her as she had the others, and Sandy had come to the conclusion that it had to do with her being pregnant.

She had heard Joan mention the word *mine* on more than one occasion. And Sandy had also endured the woman's mouth touching on her abdomen.

If Sandy was right about Joan, and she prayed to God she was, then Joan wanted Sandy's unborn baby. Which happened to be why she hadn't hurt Sandy any more than she had.

Joan had also fed Sandy, and as far as Sandy could tell, she hadn't fed the others.

When Sandy had displeased her in some way, Joan would take out her rage on one of the others. Namely, Reggie.

Sandy knew in that moment what she had to do. And though her mind rebelled against it, it was the only way to save Mindy and Reggie…

Chapter Twenty-Three

Sandy awoke to the sound of the door being thrown open. She forced herself to remain in a ball, when everything inside her screamed to cower in the corner.

Joan stepped into the room, mask in place, wearing a light-green robe with matching slippers. She made a terrifying sight to be sure.

"Oh God," Mindy moaned from her position on the other side of the room.

Sandy pretended not to notice, her gaze remaining locked on Joan's mask-covered face. She needed to do something to draw Joan's focus away from Mindy and on to her.

Lifting her head, Sandy softly whispered, "You're back..."

Joan's glittering gaze shifted from behind that mask to land on Sandy's huddled form. She stood there without moving, sending Sandy's already anxious nerves into a frenzy.

And then, the monster spoke. "Get up."

Sandy didn't want to get up, but she knew she had no choice. She threw her legs over the side of the bed and slowly got to her feet.

"Now, get upstairs," Joan demanded in that low, raspy voice of hers.

Sandy fought the urge to cover her nakedness, to run, to scream, but instead, she left her arms hanging at her sides and walked past Joan to the hall beyond.

She could feel the sicko's eyes on her back as she made her way up the stairs to open the door.

Sandy stepped inside the blessed warmth of the brightly lit kitchen and waited for Joan to tell her what to do next.

"Back to the room on the left."

Doing as Joan ordered, Sandy trailed off toward the room, grateful for the heat in the upper part of the house. It hurt her heart to know that Mindy remained behind in that freezing cold basement.

Sandy stopped at the foot of the bed without looking behind her to see if Joan had followed. She didn't need to look; she could *feel* her there, staring a hole into her nude back.

"May I use the bathroom?"

Joan took so long to answer that Sandy thought for sure she would deny her. But then she said, "Make it quick."

Sandy hurried into the bathroom and relieved herself with Joan watching. As mortifying as that was, it didn't come close to what she knew awaited her in the next room.

Flushing the toilet, Sandy slowly washed her hands. Anything to delay her going back to that bedroom.

"Thank you," she meekly murmured once she'd finished her handwashing.

Joan was suddenly in her face, her glittering eyes piercing Sandy's very soul. "Get on the bed."

Sandy wanted to cry, to call out in hopes that someone would hear her, but she didn't. Not only would Joan likely kill her then and there, but she would kill Reggie and Mindy as well.

With survival motivating her every move, Sandy whispered, "Okay," and then moved back to the bedroom to climb onto that bed.

But Joan didn't join her, nor did she chain her. She simply stood there, watching Sandy in silence for what felt like an eternity.

The words that finally came from behind that mask were far from what Sandy expected.

"Why would you want to terminate your pregnancy? And do not think to lie to me."

Sandy opened her mouth to tell Joan once again that she'd had no intention of terminating her pregnancy, but something held her back. If she thought to get anywhere with the psycho standing before her, she needed to play by said psycho's rules.

Forcing a calmness she didn't feel, Sandy licked her lips and lied. "Terminating the baby wasn't what I wanted. It was what my husband wanted."

It hurt to speak the words aloud, but speak them she did. She only prayed it had the desired effect she needed it to.

Joan shifted her weight, a move Sandy realized showed uncertainty.

"You lie."

Sandy shook her head, allowing the tears riding behind her eyes to surface. She needed to do some fast talking if she expected Joan to believe her. "I wish it were a lie. Clark already has two kids with a previous girlfriend. He doesn't want more children. I-I just didn't know what else to do."

"And your first thought was to destroy your own child? No man is worth that!"

Sandy could feel the rage coming from Joan. She had to do something and fast before the psycho woman cut her throat.

"You're right," Sandy softly admitted, feeling her way blindly through the haze of emotion Joan exuded. "No man is worth that. And no matter what I said in a moment of desperation, I would never have harmed my baby. Whatever happens to me from here on out, you can go on believing that's the truth." And it was.

Joan stared down at Sandy for long moments as if weighing the validity of her words. Without warning, she grabbed Sandy's hand and cuffed her left wrist to the bedpost. "Get comfortable. I'll be back later with food."

Sandy watched her go in silence. She waited until the door closed behind Joan before allowing her emotions free rein. She had bought herself some time. Or had she?

Joan wouldn't be easy to fool. The woman was a cold-blooded killer, one who'd managed to remain hidden for over two years, probably longer. All the while snatching kids from the very school where she worked. Joan had to be intelligent and crafty to stay under the radar like she had.

She'd killed at least five people that Sandy knew of and had two more in her basement now. Yet, the FBI and police remained clueless to the fact that their killer was actually a female. If and when they realized they were dealing with a woman, and hopefully caught this monster, Sandy and the others would likely turn up in the same woods as the previous victims.

Not if I can help it, Sandy thought, determined to survive. *No matter what I have to do to get out of this Hellhole, I will get out!*

Chapter Twenty-Four

Joan returned approximately an hour later, carrying a tray in her hands. She rounded the side of the bed that Sandy happened to be chained to and ordered, "Sit up."

Sandy hated more than anything to obey, knowing the blanket would fall, and her breasts would be exposed. But hunger and fear drove her to do exactly that.

She pushed to a sitting position, keeping her gaze lowered while Joan adjusted the tray on her lap.

Sandy's stomach growled on cue the second the aroma of food reached her senses.

She peered down at the tray's contents to find a hamburger and French fries, along with a glass of milk resting there.

"Eat up," Joan demanded, taking a seat on the side of the bed.

Sandy wanted more than anything for the freak to leave the room and let her eat without an audience. But of course, that didn't happen.

Shut her out, Sandy silently chanted, eating the food without tasting it. She felt hungrier than she'd ever been in her life.

Joan rested her palm on the inside of Sandy's left thigh and began to squeeze and release the tender flesh there. "Tell me more about Clark."

It ripped Sandy's heart in half to speak a negative word about her beloved husband, but given the circumstances, she would do what needed doing.

She wiped her mouth with the back of her hand and met the masked gaze of a psychotic Joan. "He has a two-hundred-acre ranch that was left to him by his father, and —"

"He doesn't work an outside job?" Joan interrupted, cutting off the rest of Sandy's words.

"No, he works the ranch." Sandy wanted to scream at her that Clark worked harder than any man she'd ever known, but she held her tongue.

Joan continued to knead the inside of Sandy's thigh, almost painfully. "How old is he?"

"Thirty-five."

"So, he's ten years older than you." It wasn't a question.

Sandy didn't miss the fact that Joan knew her age. And why wouldn't she? The monster worked at the high school. If Sandy had had any doubts, they were gone now.

"Yes," Sandy innocently replied.

The massaging of Sandy's thigh grew in intensity. "Why would he marry someone so young and not expect to have children with them? It makes no sense."

Sandy's insides grew cold. Joan wasn't buying her attempted deception.

The hand on Sandy's thigh slowed its movement until it stopped altogether.

Joan removed the tray from Sandy's lap, placing it on the nightstand. "Lie back."

Sandy swallowed back her fear and disgust, slid her hips down lower on the bed, and laid her head against the pillow.

Instead of closing her eyes to block out Joan's terrifyingly masked face, she stared up at the holes housing the insane-looking eyes and relaxed her body as much as her trembling muscles would allow.

Joan began coasting her palms up and down Sandy's sides. "How far along are you in your pregnancy?"

Though Joan's voice came out in a whispery rasp, it had a certain singsong sound to it that made Sandy's skin crawl.

"I-I honestly don't know. I had only just found out for certain right before..." Her words trailed off, realizing what she'd nearly said.

"Right before I found you on the side of the road, attempting to change a flat tire?"

Sandy nodded, refusing to break eye contact.

Joan's hand slid up higher along Sandy's thigh until the tips of her fingers were caressing her most vulnerable place.

Sandy wanted to clamp her legs shut, to grab that knife she knew Joan had in her robe pocket and stab her repeatedly in the chest. But she couldn't. So she lay there, helpless and still.

"Do you like that?" Joan crooned, her eyes glittering from the holes of her mask.

Sandy knew if she said yes that Joan would pick up on her lie instantly. So, she improvised. "I-I've never been with anyone other than Clark."

That gave the psycho pause. Her fingers stilled, but she didn't pull back. "You saved yourself for that garbage?"

Sandy fought the panic building inside her, her attempts at remaining calm growing harder by the second. "My-my parents raised me to believe in the sanctity of marriage. I wanted to wait for the right one."

"And you thought Clark was the right one?" Joan prompted, her fingers beginning to move once more.

"I thought so at the time." Sandy turned her head away to face the wall, a move that seemed to elicit the desired effect.

The fingers stilled again. "What do you mean by that?"

"Nothing," Sandy whispered, allowing her tears to gather and fall. If she planned to gain that psychopath's trust, then she needed to keep her wits about her and pray the woman believed her words.

And just like that, Joan's hands were suddenly gone. She jumped to her feet and had Sandy blindfolded before she could suck in a startled breath.

With her sight taken from her, Sandy felt anxiety and fear once again build to monumental levels. Being unable to see had to be the most vulnerable position a person could find themselves in. And Sandy was no exception.

Joan instantly climbed over the top of Sandy's terrified form, leaving Sandy zero doubt about what would come next.

Chapter Twenty-Five

Sandy's blindfold had been removed long ago, yet she continued to stare blindly at the wall.

She couldn't summon the energy it took to care about her surroundings. She'd been violated by that maniac…for hours.

Her mind seemed oddly blank as if unable to form a coherent thought. She could hear the television playing in the background but couldn't seem to process the words.

Hot tears burned behind her eyes, but for some reason, they refused to expel.

Sandy continued to lie there, unmoving, unfeeling, when her mind shifted to Clark and the home they shared together — a home Sandy had dreamed of raising their children in someday.

And then, a memory drifted through her mind, of something she'd told Joan in a moment of panic. *"Clark already has two kids with a previous girlfriend. He doesn't want more children."*

What if Joan decided to check into Sandy's story? What if she were now at the ranch, attempting a show of support in Clark's time of grief?

Clark wouldn't think anything of it. Neither would the police. They were looking for a man, a serial killer, murdering young girls. Not a woman who worked for the school system.

An image of Marcy Baker, the eleventh-grade English teacher with her introverted demeanor and long dresses, flashed behind Sandy's eyes.

Sandy had noticed Marcy watching her in the teacher's lounge on more than one occasion during lunch. Though the woman's glances had made Sandy uncomfortable, she'd blown it off as an introverted personality.

Now, she wasn't so sure.

The news anchorwoman's voice drifted in and out of Sandy's subconscious the longer she lay there, looking at that wall, until something she said grabbed Sandy's attention.

"Mr. Patterson is offering a two-hundred-thousand-dollar reward for any information leading to his wife's whereabouts."

Sandy rolled over to face the television, her ears straining to hear any information on Clark and her disappearance.

"Sandy Patterson was last seen leaving Harden's Drugstore in Montgomery, Alabama, a little before five o'clock pm on Friday. Her car was later discovered on Old Mill Road, parked in a ditch with a flat tire, her cell phone and purse still inside."

The disjointed sensation of hearing the woman speak of her, asking for the public's help in locating her, slid through Sandy in a bizarre feeling of surrealness.

"*The police are unsure at this time,*" the anchorwoman continued, "*if Sandy Patterson's disappearance is in any way related to the recent murders of girls in the area, but the FBI are definitely not ruling it out. They are looking into every scenario possible.*"

The door opened, and Joan stepped into the room, of course wearing that hideous leather mask and the same green robe she'd worn earlier.

She rounded Sandy's bed and uncuffed her wrist. "Come."

Both mentally and physically exhausted, Sandy climbed from the bed and moved to the door.

"Head below," Joan demanded, only this time tossing a blanket across Sandy's arm.

Sandy did as instructed, arriving at the door to her prison in the basement a moment later. She opened it and stepped inside.

Mindy still lay in her previous position, on her back, her arms and legs restrained. Only this time, she didn't look to see who'd entered. Her eyes remained closed and her body still as death.

Sandy's heart flipped over. "I-is she…" She couldn't finish the words.

"Dead?" Joan offered when Sandy simply stood there, terrified of the answer. "No, but I imagine she wants to be."

Unable to process the callous, unfeeling words coming from Joan's mouth, Sandy turned to face her. "Why are you doing this?"

"Doing what? Ridding the world of the spoiled, goodie-two-shoes twits who throw their lives away for the attention of some…man?"

The venomous words spewing from Joan's mouth were matched only by the evidence of her rage. And that evidence was across the room, battered and bruised, and barely alive.

"You'll stay in here today," Joan went on in a singsong voice, as if she hadn't just displayed a psychotic outburst. "I'll be back to get you this evening. Now, get some sleep." She turned and left, closing the door behind her.

Sandy could hear two locks click into place, the knob and the deadbolt, telling her that there would be no escape.

However, the monster had thankfully left the light on once again.

Rushing across the room, Sandy covered Mindy's nude and freezing body with the blanket Joan had allowed her to have.

Mindy's eyelids lifted a crack, her unfocused gaze seeking out Sandy. A soft moan left her throat, her lips moving without sound.

"Don't try to talk," Sandy whispered, unable to stop the tears from trickling down her cheeks.

The moan came again, followed by the barest movement of Mindy's lips.

Sandy knew without asking that Mindy attempted to tell her something. She turned her head to the side and rested her ear not an inch above Mindy's mouth.

"K...kill me..."

Sandy jerked back as if burned to stare down at the young girl in horror.

"What?" Sandy rasped through her tears. "No, Mindy. We're getting out of here, you and me. Do you understand? I'll get you out. I promise!"

Mindy's eyes rolled around in their sockets before focusing on Sandy once more. "Please..."

Sandy surged upright, her arms quickly wrapping around her middle. She turned away, attempting to block out Mindy's pleading eyes. But they had already burned a hole in Sandy's brain, and she would never be able to forget.

Chapter Twenty-Six

Sandy jerked awake, unsure of how long she'd slept. She only knew that the temperature in the room was nearly colder than her body could stand.

She threw her legs over the side of the bed, glancing longingly at the blanket covering Mindy's form.

Unable to bring herself to take the blanket from the suffering girl, Sandy began to pace. She rubbed her palms vigorously up and down her arms in an attempt to create a modicum of warmth, to no avail. Nothing she did would stave off the cold.

She wondered if Reggie was still alive, or if like Rhonda, he'd been killed and disposed of.

Making her way over to the wall, Sandy leaned in close and called out to him. "Reggie?"

When no answer came, she tried again, "Reggie!"

The door behind her opened to admit the mask-covered Joan. "Reggie is no longer with us."

Sandy slapped a hand over her mouth to prevent the cry rushing into her throat. The monster standing before her had killed Reggie.

Joan didn't remark. Instead, her gaze swung in Mindy's direction a second before she marched into the room and stopped next to the young girl's bed.

"This is not hers," Joan snarled, yanking the blanket free of Mindy and tossing it to Sandy. "Now, get upstairs."

It ripped Sandy's heart out to take the only warmth that Mindy had.

Joan tugged a knife from the pocket of the dress she wore and slowly dragged it across Mindy's cheek.

The sound that exploded from Sandy ricocheted throughout the room to drown out Mindy's cry. "Please, Joan! Please, I'm begging you not to hurt her anymore. God, please..."

Joan slowly cranked her head in Sandy's direction. "You cry for this worthless trash?"

"She's not trash, Joan. Mindy's just a young girl, a girl who's barely even lived!"

"Mindy?" Joan repeated in a deadly soft voice, bending to cut into another piece of the girl's face. "Is that what she told you? Reba lies. She always lies."

Sandy absorbed Mindy's tormented moans as if they were her own, painful and unending. Yet through it all, one thing registered in Sandy's brain. *Reba.* Joan had referred to Mindy as Reba.

Leaving the half-dead Mindy lying in a pool of her own blood, Joan stormed in Sandy's direction, knife in hand. "Move."

Sandy stumbled back a step, wrapping the blanket around her nakedness. She hurried out the door and up the stairs.

"Sit," Joan demanded when Sandy emerged in the kitchen.

Unsure of what Joan intended, Sandy approached the table in front of her and pulled out a chair. She kept quiet, taking a seat while Joan rounded the table and opened a stainless-steel refrigerator.

Joan placed the knife in her pocket and took out the makings for a sandwich, not bothering to wash the blood from her hands.

Once she'd built a turkey sandwich, she set it in front of Sandy. "Eat."

Sandy lowered her gaze to the food Joan expected her to eat, noticing a smear of blood on the edge of the bread. Her stomach lurched.

"I said eat," Joan hissed, watching Sandy closely.

With trembling hands, Sandy picked up the sandwich and bit into the side free of blood. Chewing as quickly as possible, Sandy forced herself to swallow. Her stomach lurched again. "I'm going to be sick."

"If you waste that food," Joan bit out, moving to Sandy's side, "you won't get anything else to eat."

Sandy's hands shook so badly she could barely get the sandwich back to her mouth. She closed her eyes and took another bite, fighting the need to vomit.

"Very good. Now, when you finish that, you can have some water." Joan moved back to the counter next to the fridge and set about making her own sandwich.

Sandy ate through a haze of numbness and nausea, her gaze boring into Joan's back. If not for the child Sandy carried in her womb, she would risk death and charge the maniac where she stood.

Sandy reached down with her free hand and rested her palm over her still-flat abdomen. She would find a way out of that place, no matter what she had to do to achieve it.

Keeping her gaze locked on Joan's robe-covered back, Sandy forced the rest of her food down, taking slow, deep breaths in order to *keep* it down. The next words she spoke sickened her as much as that bloody sandwich had.

"I know you're probably tired, but would you mind if I took another shower?"

Joan stiffened but didn't turn around. "Why?"

Swallowing with difficulty, Sandy whispered, "I just thought if you were going to touch me tonight, I should be clean."

Joan slowly turned to face her. "What makes you think I want to touch you?"

"I just thought—"

"You're not here to think," Joan hissed, cutting off Sandy's attempt at getting inside her head.

Moving over to a cabinet to her left, Joan yanked it open and pulled down a plastic cup. She filled it with water from the sink and placed it on the table. "Drink."

Sandy picked up the cup and brought it to her lips, her mind going to Mindy and how thirsty the young girl had to be. She wouldn't survive much longer without water. She'd already been there for two days.

Finishing off the drink, Sandy set her cup down, her gaze following Joan and every move she made.

Once Joan finished eating, she washed Sandy's cup, replaced it in the cabinet, and moved back to Sandy's side. "Go to the room."

More nausea threatened. Sandy knew what would happen in that room, what always happened in that room.

She got to her feet, tugging her blanket with her, and trailed off in the direction of the room of horrors.

Once inside, Joan ordered Sandy to lie on the bed while she cuffed Sandy's wrist in the same fashion as before.

Sandy knew what she had to do if she expected to escape that place alive.

Pushing all other thoughts from her mind, Sandy waited on the inevitable blindfold and the unwanted, disgusting touch of Joan's hands.

Only this time, Sandy wouldn't resist.

The bed dipped with Joan's weight, and her breath soon fanned out over Sandy's face. "Say it."

Sandy knew without asking what Joan wanted to hear. She reached up with her free hand, slowly cupped the back of Joan's mask-covered head, and whispered, "I love you."

With a gentle tug, she brought Joan's head toward her own.

Joan's lips settled over Sandy's, but not before a soft moan slipped free.

Sandy knew that she'd somehow reached the psychotic fiend. Her willing submission had affected Joan in more ways than one... She'd heard it in that moan, felt it in Joan's kiss.

Hardening her emotions, Sandy did what must be done in order to survive. Though she knew she would never be the same once she escaped that place, she would save her unborn child and return to Clark. Even if she had to sell her soul to do it. And in a sense, that's exactly what she did.

Chapter Twenty-Seven

Sandy lay beneath Joan, unmoving and unfeeling. She had gone past the point of no return by giving herself completely to the monster lying on top of her.

Joan had forced her to do things before, but Sandy hadn't needed to be ordered or coaxed this time. No, she'd touched, caressed, and convinced the monster of her growing attraction to her. Or so, she prayed.

Joan lifted her head but remained on top of Sandy's body. "As good as that felt to me, do you really expect me to believe you felt it too?"

For once, Sandy was grateful for the blindfold that hid the disgust she knew swam in her eyes.

Instead of responding, she reached up, took hold of the fiend's hand, and guided it between their bodies. "You tell me."

It took everything Sandy had not to tighten up with the feel of Joan's fingers touching her.

The fingers were suddenly gone as was Joan's weight.

A rustling sound could be heard coming from the side of the bed, and then Sandy's blindfold was removed.

Joan stood there naked, wearing nothing but that horrid mask. She leaned in and unlocked Sandy's wrist. "You can take a shower now. If you disappoint me, I'll return you to the basement with Reba, where you can watch her suffer."

Sandy kept her expression as passive as possible while crawling to the edge of the mattress. "How come you hate Reba so much?"

Joan's head twitched. Wearing that mask, the sudden tic made her appear even more horrific. "What do you know about Reba?"

Suddenly terrified once more, Sandy's mind scrambled around to think of a response. "Nothing more than the fact that she's trash."

The crack of Joan's palm across Sandy's face sent her toppling over backward. The sting of that blow brought tears to Sandy's eyes.

Joan was instantly on top of her, a knife to her throat. "I better not ever hear you speak of her in such a way again! Ever!"

Sandy was about to die. She knew it as surely as she knew the eyes staring down at her through the mask holes belonged to someone manic and unreachable.

But she had to try. "I'm sorry, Joan! It was jealousy that made me say that. I shouldn't have said it. I-I had no right. Please don't be angry with me. Not after the beautiful time we just shared together."

The maniac didn't move for several heartbeats, that knife still pressed to Sandy's throat. And then, the blade lifted slightly. "You don't need to be jealous. Especially of *her*. Now, go shower."

And just like that, Joan pushed to her feet and left the room, leaving Sandy to wonder what had just happened.

* * * *

Sandy sat propped up on the bed, her gaze glued to the television, hoping—praying—for news that the FBI was getting close to finding her abductor. But nothing had been said so far.

Over the next several hours, Joan wandered in and out of the room, bringing Sandy an occasional drink until she eventually took her back to the basement.

It didn't take a rocket scientist for Sandy to figure out Joan's schedule. She brought Sandy to the upper floor in the evenings when she was sure to be home and returned her to the basement when she left for work, to ensure Sandy couldn't be heard or hope to escape.

Wrapping her blanket tightly around her shoulders, Sandy entered the small prison room of the basement and waited for the door to close and lock behind her.

Once assured that Joan had left, Sandy hurried across the room to Mindy's side.

Mindy's face was ghost white and from the stillness of her body, she couldn't possibly be alive.

"Oh God, no," Sandy choked out, lowering to her knees and placing her ear over Mindy's mouth.

A small amount of breath could be felt.

Dizzy with relief, Sandy freed the blanket from her shoulders and covered Mindy's freezing form.

"Mindy?"

The young girl remained completely still.

"Mindy, please hold on!"

Sandy began to vigorously rub her palms up and down Mindy's arms while attempting to avoid any wounds she encountered in the process.

She worked on Mindy's legs next and then quickly covered her with the blanket.

Though the young girl continued to breathe, she never moved or made a sound.

Sandy sat back on her haunches on that ice-cold concrete floor, unable to take her gaze from Mindy's mutilated face.

"*God*," Sandy began, her voice a tormented whisper. "*Please help us. I don't deserve to be here any more than Mindy does. I've prayed, gone to church my entire life, and have never purposely hurt anyone. I'm begging you to help us!*"

Yet, the harder Sandy prayed, the more hopeless she felt. God wasn't going to save her, any more than he would save poor Mindy Reyes.

With a cry of desolation, Sandy jumped to her feet and began to do the only other thing she knew to stay warm... Pace.

Chapter Twenty-Eight

Sandy alternated between shivering on her twin bed and pacing a path along the concrete floor of her prison.

She consistently checked on Mindy, making sure she still breathed, but the young, tortured girl never moved.

"Mindy?" she called out, hoping that if Mindy could somehow hear her voice, she would hold on until help arrived.

Stumbling over to Mindy's bed, Sandy felt once more for signs of breath, but no air expelled from the girl's mouth.

"No, no, no, no." Sandy wept, her hands trembling so badly she could barely grab onto the edge of the blanket.

She yanked the covering free and threw her leg over Mindy's chained, naked body.

"Breathe!" she gasped, placing her palms against Mindy's chest. "Come on, breathe!" She began chest compressions.

Sandy's mind couldn't comprehend what was happening. How long had she been doing chest compressions and breathing into Mindy's mouth? She didn't know. Nothing mattered to Sandy in that moment but feeling the girl's breath, hearing her heart beating once again.

Exhaustion soon took over, and Sandy's arms finally gave out. She laid on top of Mindy's dead body and simply…wept.

She wept for a life that had been snuffed out far too soon. She wept for Reggie, for Rhonda, and all the others who'd suffered and died at the hands of a monster.

The sound of locks turning on the door caught Sandy's attention. She barely had time to lift her head before Joan's enraged face came into view.

"What have you done?" Joan snarled, racing across the floor of that basement and wrapping her hands in Sandy's hair.

Sandy cried out at the force with which Joan jerked her sideways, sending her slamming against the unforgiving concrete of the floor.

"Reba?" Joan whispered, smacking the dead girl's face. But of course, Mindy remained unmoving.

Sandy scrambled back, terrified and on the verge of making a break for that open door. When a thought settled over her like a warm blanket.

She wasn't sure who Reba was to Joan, but she had obviously made a huge impact on the maniac's life.

Sandy's gaze touched on Mindy's long dark hair, and she remembered the pretty green of Mindy's eyes, eyes so like Rhonda Shivers'. The same hair as Rhonda's too. In fact, all the girls that Joan had killed resembled one another. If Sandy happened to be right in her thinking, she'd bet that this Reba, whoever she was, had dark hair and green eyes as well. And she meant something to Joan.

Pushing unsteadily to her feet, Sandy blurted, "I killed her."

Joan's head twitched in that insane way that Sandy had only witnessed once before. And it terrified her.

With the knife suddenly in her hand, Joan began to move in Sandy's direction. "You killed her?"

As terrified as that mask happened to be, it didn't hold a candle to the menacing sound of Joan's whisper-soft voice.

This is it, Sandy thought, instinctively backing up a step. *It'll either work, or I'll die right alongside Mindy.*

"I had to."

Joan's head twitched again.

"You loved her!" Sandy nearly shouted, her entire body trembling in fear. "I could see that you loved her."

Another head twitch from Joan.

Sandy was beginning to panic. What if she'd guessed incorrectly in assuming that Reba was someone important to Joan? "I'm sorry if what I did was wrong, but I knew how you felt about her…"

"You —" Twitch "You're jealous?"

Lowering her hands to a nonthreatening position, Sandy lifted her chin, which was no easy feat, considering she half expected Joan to spring on her with that knife. "Yes."

Joan didn't move nor did the blade she held in a white-knuckled grip. "I don't believe you."

Sandy was sure that Joan could see her terrified heart beating behind her ribs. "It's the truth. I don't want it to be, but it is."

Joan's head twitched inside that mask a few more times and then without warning, she sprang forward and buried the blade of that knife into Sandy's shoulder.

Disbelief warred with reality inside Sandy's stunned, spinning brain. Reality won out. Joan hadn't believed her confession of jealousy and had stabbed her in retaliation.

Sandy had no doubts that she would die soon. Her only regret was that she never got the chance to tell Clark about the baby they'd created, to look into his eyes when he realized he would be a father.

That would never happen now. Sandy would die in that basement, and she would never see her precious husband again.

Her world turned black...

Chapter Twenty-Nine

Pain. So much pain. Was she in Hell?

Sandy attempted to open her eyes, realizing very quickly that her previous blindfold was back in place. Which meant that she was alive. Joan hadn't killed her.

Did that mean that Joan had believed her confession of jealousy? Probably not, but the possibility gave Sandy a spark of hope.

Another realization dawned. She was in bed, a warm bed, and she wasn't restrained.

She cleared her parched throat. "Joan?"

Footsteps echoed nearby, and a moment later, the blindfold was removed.

Sandy blinked a few times to clear her vision, the pain in her shoulder nearly too much to bear. "It hurts."

She peered up at the eyeholes in Joan's mask, praying to God the insane woman didn't plan on stabbing her again.

Joan reached into the pocket of her robe and withdrew a few pills. She placed them on the nightstand next to a glass of water. "Take those."

Sandy glanced at the pills, her heart pounding anew.

"It's only acetaminophen," Joan snapped, plucking up the pills and water. "If I were going to kill you, I would have done it in the basement."

Pushing herself up to a sitting position, Sandy bit back a groan from the pain in her shoulder and held out her hand.

Joan handed her the pills and then the water. "You will stay in this room until your wound heals. If you attempt to leave or make any noise whatsoever, it won't bode well for you."

Sandy knew that Joan would kill her in an instant. The woman was a powder keg of insanity. She could blow at any moment.

Thinking her words over carefully, Sandy took her pills, washing them down with the water, and then met Joan's gaze once again. The maniac hadn't killed her, which meant that somewhere deep in her psyche, she wanted to believe Sandy cared for her.

"I won't try to leave."

Joan gave a sharp nod and turned to go.

"Will you stay with me for a little longer?" Sandy was surprised by the steadiness of her voice in the face of her fear. And as much as she hated speaking those words aloud, she had no choice. Not if she hoped to convince Joan to trust her.

Joan hesitated. "Why?"

Why indeed? "I'm afraid…"

"Afraid of what?"

Think, Sandy! "Of losing my baby."

"You mean *my* baby," Joan shot back in a deadly soft tone. "The baby is fine. Now, keep your mouth shut. I have things to do."

So, Joan planned on keeping her baby. *Over my dead body.*

Then another thought filtered in through the madness. If Joan wanted Sandy's unborn child, that meant she had no intention of killing her. She planned to keep Sandy alive, at least until the birth.

Sandy couldn't imagine spending the next eight months of her life in captivity. Especially in the clutches of a psychopath like Joan.

No, Sandy would find a way to escape, and soon. No matter what she had to do to make that happen.

* * * *

The next week crawled by at a snail's pace, with Sandy being locked in the basement by day and permitted to return to the upper floor in the evenings.

Joan had removed Mindy's body the same day she'd stabbed Sandy. Reggie had obviously been disposed of as well, since Sandy hadn't heard anything coming from that room in the last eight days.

Her heart ached for the two teens, whose lives had been taken from them in the vilest, cruelest ways imaginable. Just as the others had…

Sandy was permitted to watch television in the evenings after Joan arrived home and freed her from the basement. But the local news stations hadn't mentioned anything about finding the bodies of Mindy or Reggie. Which Sandy found strange.

Rhonda's and Heidi Birch's bodies had been dumped where they would be easily discovered. As had Louann Henderson, Maryann Jones, and Destiny Murray. And the police, with the help of the FBI, were out searching for Reggie and Mindy day and night, and so far, had found nothing.

Had Joan actually dumped them, as per her usual, or were they somewhere still in the house?

Sandy shivered.

Chapter Thirty

Sandy stared blindly at the dresser across the room, her wrist once again chained to the bedpost.

Joan had brought her upstairs immediately upon her return that evening.

The psycho had entered the basement, wearing that leather mask, her movements jerky and quick, demanding Sandy hurry. Of course, Sandy didn't speak for fear of angering her.

Joan had fed her, allowed her to use the bathroom, and then left her chained in the upstairs bedroom. She'd then turned on the television before leaving.

Sandy had watched her go, imagining all the ways she'd like to kill her. Sandy prayed she would get the chance to not only end the monster's existence but to torture her slowly before she died.

She would chain Joan to that twin bed in the basement and beat and terrorize her the way she'd beaten and terrorized those young high school girls. And Reggie...

Sandy squeezed her eyes closed, hoping to dispel the dark images her mind had created. She felt crazy, as if she were in someone else's body, unable to pull back from the abyss.

Her thoughts suddenly turned to Clark and her parents. They had to think her dead by now. She'd been missing for two weeks.

No, she silently whispered, Clark wouldn't give up looking for her. Of that, Sandy was certain. She had never known anyone as strong and determined as Clark. He would search for her until his dying breath, or until, God forbid, her body turned up in a wooded area somewhere.

But Joan wanted Sandy's baby, which meant that Sandy still had time. She hoped.

A crash sounded from somewhere in the kitchen, sending Sandy scrambling back against the headboard.

The shattering of dishes came next, leaving little doubt in Sandy's terrified mind that Joan was in a rage.

What had happened in the last hour to cause such an outburst?

The crashing sounds stopped as quickly as they'd come, and Joan's masked face suddenly appeared in the doorway. She held that black baton in her hand.

Sandy's insides turned to ice. By the stiff stance of the robe-covered psycho, it was clear that her intentions were definitely not good.

She stepped deeper in the room, pulling a knife from the pocket of her robe. "Get on your stomach."

Sandy began to tremble, her terror consuming her to the point of hysteria. "Joan, please! Whatever I did, I'm—"

"I said get on your stomach!"

Sandy's teeth began to chatter, but she did as Joan demanded. After the insane woman's attack last week in that basement, Sandy wasn't willing to risk being stabbed again.

She rolled to her stomach, her head turned in Joan's direction. As much as she hated looking at that knife clutched in Joan's hand, Sandy couldn't bring herself to look away.

Joan set about chaining Sandy's other wrist and her ankles to the bedposts, muttering words that made little sense. And then she snarled, "It's your fault. All of it!"

Sandy had no idea what that meant, and she was far too afraid to ask.

When the silence in the room grew deafening, Sandy opened her mouth to say something—anything to bring Joan back into her field of vision. The not knowing what was about to happen only heightened her terror.

Just then, something came down on the calf of her leg. Hard.

Sandy cried out, the pain of the blow spreading through her body like fire.

Joan had hit her with the baton.

Another blow to her thigh came next and then another, until Sandy's cries turned into agonized screams.

"Shut up!" Joan growled in a voice that didn't sound human.

She was suddenly back at Sandy's side. "Open."

Sandy blinked up at Joan through her tears, terrified to the point where she parted her chattering teeth on cue.

Joan shoved what looked to be a sock inside Sandy's mouth before she could pull away and then immediately went back to swinging that baton.

She beat Sandy's legs, feet, and arms until she nearly passed out from the pain. Just when she thought she could take no more, Joan did the unthinkable. She sodomized her with the baton.

A hoarse, agonizing scream ripped from Sandy's throat, muffled only by that sock in her mouth.

She wrapped her fingers around the chains binding her arms and fought with everything she had to break free. But the chains held... And the torture continued.

Chapter Thirty-One

Fingers caressed Sandy's cheek, dragging softly and slowly along her jaw.

The sock was pulled from her mouth, and Joan's mask-covered face appeared in her vision. "I didn't enjoy doing that, Sandy, but you shouldn't have upset me."

Sandy could barely think beyond the pain radiating throughout her body. Joan was apologizing to her. She'd tormented Sandy for what felt like forever, only to suddenly grow a conscience?

Sandy wanted to lash out, to beg Joan to end her torment. Nothing mattered to her anymore, not Clark, her parents, or even her own life.

But then, her mind settled on her unborn baby, a baby she silently prayed still lived. And if Sandy hoped to give her child a chance to be born, a chance to actually live, she had to be careful of her reaction to the monster sitting next to her.

Gathering every ounce of strength she had left, Sandy peeled her eyes open and licked her dry, swollen lips. "I'm...sorry."

Joan's head tilted to the side. She lifted her hand and gently tucked some of Sandy's hair behind her ear. "You won't let it happen again?"

Sandy had no idea what she'd done to enrage Joan to begin with, but she whispered, "I won't."

"Good girl," Joan crooned before releasing Sandy's wrists and ankles from her bonds.

She then grabbed a blanket and covered Sandy's naked body. "I'm going to be home for a few days, so I'll be here to take care of you. Try to get some rest."

Joan left the room without closing the door behind her.

Once assured that Joan wasn't near, Sandy buried her face in her pillow and released a moan of agony that felt as if it came from her very soul.

The knife wound in her shoulder didn't compare to the pain in her arms and legs. Nor the assault from that baton.

Sandy wanted to die. Joan had stripped her of all humanity, had laid her bare and stolen her will to live. Almost...

No matter what happened to Sandy, she would ensure that her child survived.

She attempted to roll over, but the agonizing burn deep inside her limbs forced her to remain unmoving.

All too soon, Joan's masked face appeared in Sandy's vision once again. She held something in her hands, but Sandy couldn't make out what it was.

"Lie still," Joan soothed, the sickening sound of her voice sliding over Sandy's trembling form like an oily film. "This will help you to feel better."

Joan began to busy herself with the contents in her hands and then leaned over Sandy.

The cool feel of some sort of cream touched Sandy's arm. It took her a second to realize that Joan attempted to rub a substance into her bruised and battered skin.

"Would you like to listen to the television while I smear this salve onto you?"

Sandy couldn't believe the change in the maniac. One minute, she was beating Sandy with a baton, and the next, she attempted to soothe her with kindness?

Too afraid to flip Joan's crazy switch again, Sandy whispered, "That would be nice."

Joan quickly stood and moved across the room to the television. It came on with a flourish, spouting something about laundry detergent.

All too soon, Joan returned to Sandy's side to finish her disgusting ministrations.

"Welcome to the five o'clock news," a voice floated out from the TV. *"This is Megan Armstrong here with you this evening with an update on the Montgomery County serial killings."*

Joan's hands stilled on Sandy's back.

"The Montgomery Police Department has announced that they may have a break in the case. A sixteen-year-old girl walking home from school today was nearly abducted by a female driving a dark-blue sedan. The FBI is keeping the girl's identity from the public until further investigation. Though the police are not certain the attempted abduction is related to the previous murders in the county, they are looking into the possibility."

The anchorwoman went on to warn the public to be vigilant, explaining that the FBI were now looking into the possibility that the serial killer could be a woman. The witness also happened to remember the first letter of the sedan's tag number. M.

Without warning, Joan surged to her feet, grabbed Sandy by the arm, and yanked her up.

Sandy cried out from the pain that movement caused. She stumbled along behind Joan as the psychotic maniac dragged her through the kitchen, down the stairs, and shoved her inside the basement.

The sound of the locks clicking into place sealed Sandy's fate. But that didn't take away from the hope she felt spreading through her chest. Joan had left a witness.

In that moment, everything that had happened that afternoon fell into place for Sandy. Joan's rage, her manic actions, were due to the fact that she'd attempted to snatch another girl and failed. Not only had she failed, but that sixteen-year-old near-victim could identify her near-abductor.

The walls had to be closing in on Joan. And she knew it. Which was why her usual irrational behavior had worsened without warning. She had to be in a panic.

Realizing she'd been yanked from that room without the opportunity to grab a blanket, Sandy moved over to huddle on her twin bed.

She gingerly sat, the pain in her bottom as bad as the pain in her legs. And then she rolled into a ball, bringing her knees up to her chest and wrapping her arms around her upper body. But no amount of huddling would bring her warmth.

Chapter Thirty-Two

Sandy jerked awake to the sound of the basement door crashing open.

Joan's mask-covered face hovered in the open doorway, one hand in the hair of a terrified girl and the other holding a knife to the teenager's throat.

She shoved the girl forward. "On the bed!"

Sandy's stomach dropped in more than a little terror and disbelief. She'd thought for sure that Joan wouldn't dare snatch another victim, not with the FBI now combing the streets in search of a female driving a dark-blue sedan.

The girl's terrified cries tore at Sandy's rapidly beating heart, but there would be nothing she could do for Joan's latest victim. There never was.

Joan followed the girl to the bed and chained her down while the young teenager sobbed uncontrollably.

Backhanding the girl across the mouth, Joan snarled, "Shut up!"

She then placed the knife she held in the pocket of her dress and moved next to Sandy's bed. She held out her hand. "Come."

Afraid of what she might have to suffer next, Sandy placed her trembling palm against Joan's and stood.

But Joan didn't push or hurt her. Instead, she gently wrapped her fingers around Sandy's and led her from the room.

Once upstairs, Joan pulled out a chair from the table, offered it to Sandy, and then poured them both a cup of water.

Sandy warily picked up her cup, waiting for the other proverbial shoe to drop, and then took a drink of her water.

Joan skirted the table and sat in a chair across from her. "Tell me about your mother."

Not sure she heard her correctly, Sandy whispered, "M-my mother?"

Taking a sip of her own water, Joan nodded and then lowered her cup. "Yes. Tell me about her. What she looks like, what she smells like, how she was with you when you were younger."

What an extremely weird thing to ask, Sandy thought, lowering her gaze. She didn't want to speak of her mother to this freak. She didn't even want her mother's name to be spoken in the presence of such evil. But she had no choice and she knew it.

"I look like her," Sandy hesitantly began, conjuring up her mother's smiling face. "Only, she's much prettier than I am."

Joan made a sound in the back of her throat. "I doubt that but go on."

Sandy vaguely nodded. "All right. Mama just had her fiftieth birthday. She and my dad have been married for twenty-seven years."

"So, she was twenty-five when you were born," Joan commented, forcing Sandy's gaze back to her hidden face.

"Yes, she was."

Joan tilted her head. "Was she good to you?"

"She was always good to me," Sandy softly admitted, wondering where Joan was heading with her questions. She'd just abducted a teenager and then dragged Sandy upstairs to have a chat as if nothing were out of the ordinary. Of course, it likely wasn't in Joan's mind. She was, after all, insane.

Joan's fingers began to knead the plastic cup in front of her. "She never...touched you inappropriately?"

Disgust slid through Sandy to fight for a position among the painful throbbing of her bruised body.

She wanted to curl her top lip, to spit in the face of the nutjob sitting across from her.

Sandy was determined to escape the house of horrors she found herself in and take the girl in the basement with her. So, she lied. She forced the sickening words past her numb lips and prayed to God they were believable. "No, but my uncle did."

Joan's fingers stopped moving. "Your uncle did what?"

"He-he began touching me when I was five."

"Your mother didn't stop him?" Joan asked so softly Sandy barely heard it.

Sandy lifted her gaze. "I never told her."

"Why wouldn't you go to her?" Joan pressed, her fingers still wrapped around that plastic cup.

"Because I didn't want to hurt her. Uncle Ron was her only brother. I knew how much she loved him. I was afraid I would disappoint her and that she would hate me. So, I kept quiet."

Joan remained silent for several heartbeats, then, "How long were you molested by your uncle?"

How dare she use the word molested *after what she's done to me.* "Until I was twelve. He died before my thirteenth birthday."

Joan slowly stood and moved around the table. She leaned in and wrapped Sandy in a hug. "I would kill him for you if he were alive."

First, Joan killed teenage girls after raping and torturing them, then she abducted Sandy, holding her against her will, then raped and beat her as well. Now the quack was hugging her, wanting to avenge her for a crime that she had no idea didn't really happen.

What a nutjob, Sandy thought, not wanting to but hugging her in return.

Joan pulled back slightly and brushed her mouth across Sandy's, sending bile shooting into Sandy's throat.

She swallowed it down before it could projectile into the nutjob's face. "I wish you could have killed him too."

Joan straightened. "Do you know how many kids at the high school suffer the touch of an adult who's supposed to love them? It's always the lower-class kids. Never the popular students, cheerleaders and such."

She bent and kissed Sandy again.

Meanwhile, Sandy's mind was racing from Joan's words. She'd just given Sandy some small insight into who and what she was.

Perhaps Sandy had been wrong about Joan from the beginning. Maybe the maniac standing in front of her wasn't Miss Baker, after all. The English teacher wouldn't know the goings-on inside the homes of her students. But the guidance counselor would. Or a grief counselor.

Mrs. Tate's face flashed through Sandy's mind.

And then, Mrs. Freedman and her strong dislike of the grief counselor.

Sandy suddenly wondered about Mrs. Tate's first name. She couldn't remember ever hearing it. But she did recall the looks the counselor had received from some of the teachers at Purvis High.

Another thought struck. According to Mr. Humphreys, Mrs. Tate had been called in two years earlier after the murder of the first high school girl. Which would be a perfect coverup for the grief counselor. What better way to case out new victims than to inject yourself in the midst of them?

Chapter Thirty-Three

Sandy spent the rest of the evening suffering Joan's company as well as her disgusting touch.

The woman had continued to question Sandy about her childhood for what had to be close to an hour, and then she'd taken Sandy to the bedroom and chained her wrist to the bed.

Sandy gazed up at the post her hand was bound to, taking in the large wooden ball at the top. She'd tried on more than one occasion to wriggle the cuff over that ball, without success. No, Joan was far too crafty to chain her victims in a manner they could escape.

Joan entered the bedroom with what looked to be a robe dangling from one hand and a pistol in the other. Her movements appeared casual and nonthreatening.

Sandy had never seen her with a gun before. Was Joan going to shoot her? Sandy's heart jumped into her throat.

Joan unchained Sandy's wrist and tossed the robe onto the bed next to her. "Put this on."

Sandy wanted to ask what Joan planned to do with her, but she didn't dare, not with that gun pointed in her direction.

Easing her aching legs over the side of the bed, Sandy stood on shaky legs and donned the plain white robe.

"We're going out back," Joan informed her, taking Sandy by the hand. "If you try anything, I won't hesitate to shoot you."

Sandy's heart pounded too hard for her to speak. She nodded instead, allowing Joan to lead her through the kitchen and into a room she hadn't been in before.

A fireplace sat to the left, with dozens of trinkets resting along the top.

Sandy's gaze swept the rest of the room, taking in the brown sofa and matching recliner, a large television, and a coffee table. No pictures adorned the walls.

There were two windows in the room, both of which contained bars. A feeling of defeat was instant.

Joan pushed her toward a door with light coming through a window at the top, which Sandy quickly surmised to be the exit.

Excitement, nerves, and adrenaline exploded at once. Hopefully she would see neighbors near the house, someone — anyone — she could get the attention of.

Joan dug a set of keys from the pocket of her dress and unlocked the deadbolt. There would be no escape through that door without those keys. Sandy figured the monster had set up all the doors in the house in the same fashion to keep her prisoners locked safely inside.

Joan opened the door. "Go on."

Sandy moved cautiously forward, emerging onto a porch. She quickly glanced around to take in her surroundings, and her heart sank. There were no neighbors as far as her eyes could see.

A tall chain link fence wrapped around the backyard, enclosing it in a prison of its own. Barbed wire lined the top, with one gate on the far end, leading to freedom. A wooden bench rested beneath some trees to the right, with hummingbird feeders hanging from the branches.

The area appeared serene, like something out of a magazine. Minus the barbed wire.

"Well?" Joan murmured in that singsong voice. "Do you like it?"

Choosing her words carefully, Sandy feigned a timid nod. "It's beautiful. Did you do all this?"

"Most of it."

Sandy pretended to admire the scenery, her gaze taking in ways of escape that lay beyond the fence. From what she could gather, they were far away from civilization, with only a long, winding dirt road leading from the side of the house.

Even if Sandy could somehow manage to get through that gate without dying first, she had no idea how far away from civilization they actually were.

Her gaze strayed back to the gate.

"Go over there and sit," Joan ordered, bringing Sandy's attention back to her. "On the bench."

Grateful for the robe to ward off some of the chilly air, Sandy stepped off the porch and made her way on bare feet to the bench.

She thought about the girl chained down in that icy basement, freezing and terrified, awaiting her death. And Sandy knew the girl understood she would die. She'd seen it in the girl's eyes the moment Joan had forced her onto that bed.

Joan suddenly joined Sandy on the bench. She didn't speak at first, and then, "We have to leave this place."

Adrenaline shot through Sandy's veins once more. She wanted to ask what Joan meant by that statement, but she held her tongue and let the psycho talk. Besides, she was afraid of that gun Joan held. The woman was a ticking time bomb who could be set off by the slightest word.

Sandy sat there, staring straight ahead, the stab wound in her shoulder burning and throbbing with every beat of her heart. And she was cold to her very bones.

"My mama and brother are buried in Arkansas," Joan went on to say while Sandy burrowed deeper inside her robe to prevent the shivering from overtaking her.

"What happened to them?"

"It doesn't matter."

Sandy shifted her gaze to Joan's mask-covered profile, more than a little terrified. Something had changed in Joan's voice.

Not sure what to say next but full of questions, Sandy remained quiet, until the chattering of her teeth soon interrupted the silence between them.

Joan's head turned in her direction. "What's wrong with you?"

Afraid to answer, yet more afraid not to, Sandy admitted, "I'm freezing."

Joan's head tilted. "You're sweating."

She lifted her arm and laid the back of her hand against Sandy's forehead. "You have a fever."

Joan's hand dropped away, and she jumped to her feet. "Get inside."

Sandy quickly obeyed, hurrying back to the house, knowing that pistol was aimed at her back.

The warmth of the living room soon engulfed her, eliciting a moan of relief from Sandy's throat. Yet the shivering continued.

Chapter Thirty-Four

Sandy watched from beneath her lashes as Joan took out her keys, locked the back door, and ushered her toward the bedroom she'd previously been chained in.

But Joan didn't order Sandy to bed. Instead, she guided her to the bathroom, turned on the water to the tub, and placed a plug in the drain. "Get in."

Hating more than anything to disrobe in front of Joan again, Sandy untied the sash and lowered the material from her shoulders.

Joan took the robe from her trembling fingers and waited for Sandy to climb into the tub.

The warm water felt like Heaven on Sandy's fevered flesh. She quickly sat down, placing both of her hands beneath the continuous flow of the faucet.

"I'll be right back." Joan spun on her heel, leaving Sandy alone in the bathroom.

Sandy wanted to jump up and search the cabinet beneath the sink for a weapon, but with the water running in the tub, she couldn't listen for the psycho's return. Plus, nothing beneath that sink would do her any good against that gun.

Joan was back within seconds, holding a cup of water and some pills Sandy recognized as acetaminophen. "Take these. They'll break your fever."

Sandy accepted the offering, swallowing the medicine and handing the cup back to Joan. "Thank you."

It galled Sandy to thank the monster for anything, but Joan was beginning to trust her, even if a small amount, and Sandy needed to keep that trust if she thought to escape.

Once Joan set the cup on the counter behind her, she lowered to her knees beside the tub and reached for the bandage covering Sandy's stab wound. She peeled it back.

Sandy cried out when the tape pulled at her injured flesh. She glanced down at her throbbing shoulder, only to notice a red streak running from the knife wound along with the evidence of puss.

"It's infected," Joan practically growled, yanking the rest of the bandage off. She surged to her feet.

"Bathe and get out. The pills will break your fever, but you'll need antibiotics — antibiotics that I don't have."

Sandy's anxiety spiked again. If Joan had no antibiotics, Sandy could die from infection. And that red streak coming from her wound was running straight toward her heart.

"Hurry it up," Joan snapped, grabbing a towel from a shelf to her left.

Sandy bathed as quickly as possible, her brain fuzzy from fever, and her body aching everywhere.

She pulled the plug and stood, accepting the towel Joan offered. Heat burned behind Sandy's eyes, and the shivering in her limbs remained.

Once she finished drying herself, Joan helped her back in the robe she'd previously worn and then gripped her by the elbow.

Leading her through the bedroom, Joan snatched up a blanket and hurried toward the door.

In less than a minute, Sandy found herself back in the freezing room of the basement.

The girl chained to the bed began to beg, her green eyes swollen from crying. "Please help me!"

Joan shoved Sandy forward, shut the door, and pulled the gun from her dress pocket.

Sandy panicked. Joan was going to kill the girl if she didn't do something, and quick.

What Sandy was about to do would hurt something fierce, but given the circumstances, she would endure it. She moaned, allowed her eyes to roll shut, and dropped heavily to the concrete floor.

Joan was at her side in an instant, her palm slapping against Sandy's cheek.

Sandy moaned again, forcing her head to roll to the side.

"Don't you do this," Joan growled, smacking her harder.

Between her erratic heartbeat and the shaking in her limbs, Sandy could barely open her lips to speak. "Help...me."

Joan snarled a string of curse words, straightened, and practically ran from the basement. The door slammed behind her.

Sandy waited until she heard both locks click into place before pushing to her feet, snatching up her blanket, and hurrying to the young girl's side.

"Shhhhh," Sandy shushed her, covering her naked body with the blanket. "It's going to be okay. You're okay. What's your name?"

"Selma," the girl whispered through her tears. "Please help me!"

"I'm going to help you. Can you tell me what happened?" If Selma could give her some insight on how she ended up in the clutches of that psycho, maybe Sandy could figure out who, exactly, Joan was. Not that it would do her a lot of good, but at least she would know who she was dealing with.

"I-I'm not sure."

"Think," Sandy implored her. "Whatever you can remember might help get us out of here."

Selma's red, swollen eyes focused on a place just beyond Sandy's injured shoulder. The girl stared across the room for so long Sandy was sure she wouldn't answer.

"I checked out of school early," Selma began in a low tone, her gaze still half vacant. "I was going to meet my boyfriend at the Tastee Freeze a few blocks over from the school."

She paused for long moments.

"Go on," Sandy gently encouraged, brushing some of Selma's dark hair back from her face.

"I started walking in the direction of 3rd and Main. After crossing over Main, I stopped near a vacant lot to smoke a cigarette behind some trees where I wouldn't be seen."

More tears filled Selma's eyes. "When I made it back to the road, I saw a car idling along the curb. The back door was open on the car, and I could hear a baby crying inside. I ran over to help... And—and that's the last thing I remember." She began to sob once more.

So, that's how Joan was getting her victims, by using a child in distress as her ruse.

Chapter Thirty-Five

Sandy's chills eventually stopped, evidence that the acetaminophen had finally kicked in and broken her fever.

She stayed next to Selma as long as she felt safe to do so. If Joan returned and caught her talking to the girl, she would likely kill them both.

"I need you to listen to me, Selma, and listen good."

Selma stared pleadingly into Sandy's eyes. "Okay."

"The woman who took you is a psychopath. That means that anything you do or say can set her off. Are you with me so far?"

At Selma's nod, Sandy continued. "You may have to stay down here for a while, and —"

"No, no, no," Selma pleaded, jerking at her chains. "Please, you have to get me out of here."

Desperate not to get caught speaking with the girl, Sandy snapped, "I said I would help you and I will! But you are going to have to do exactly as I say."

Something in Sandy's tone must have reached Selma's panicked brain. She took a shuddering breath and whispered, "I'll do what you tell me. Just please don't leave me here."

"I won't leave you." Sandy glanced nervously over her shoulder. "But I am going to have to take your blanket. If she comes back and sees that I've helped you in any way, she'll kill you. Understand?"

Though Selma's tears spilled anew, she nodded her understanding.

Sandy continued. "I am going to do my best to keep her from this basement. As long as she's upstairs with me and I don't anger her, she'll leave you alone."

Selma sniffed, her gaze locked on Sandy's.

Blinking back her own tears, Sandy rushed out, "She has a set of keys in her pocket that go to the locks on your chains and also the back door. I don't know about the front. I haven't been to that part of the house. The windows have bars on them, and the backyard is surrounded by a chain link fence with barbed wire along the top. There's a lock on the gate, and I can only pray that the key is on that same set she has in her pocket."

Sandy ran a hand down her face, the movement sending pain shooting through her injured shoulder. "If I can get my hands on those keys, I can get you free of these chains, and we can make it out that back door to freedom. But none of that will happen if you don't do exactly what I told you to do."

Selma nodded through her tears. "Okay. Just please don't leave me here. I'm begging you."

"I won't leave you. I swear it."

"I'm so sorry," Sandy whispered, removing the blanket covering Selma and hurrying across the room to her own bed.

She hated more than anything to leave the young girl to freeze, but the alternative would be far worse.

Joan eventually returned, carrying a white bag in her hand. Her gaze touched on Selma before settling on Sandy. "Come."

Sandy followed Joan back upstairs to the kitchen, where a chair sat slightly away from the table.

"Sit," Joan demanded, taking down a cup and filling it with water.

She then reached inside the bag, took out a prescription bottle, and popped the lid off.

Dumping two pills into her palm, she set the bottle down and handed Sandy the pills. "It's antibiotics. You're not allergic to penicillin, are you?"

Sandy shook her head, her gaze straying to the name on that bottle. *Melissa Duggar.* "No, I'm not allergic to any medications."

"You're not supposed to take them on an empty stomach, or it'll make you sick. I'll make you a sandwich."

Attempting a grateful look, Sandy whispered her thanks and took the pills, her gaze flicking back to the name on that prescription bottle. Where had she heard it before? And then it came to her. Melissa Duggar was a student at Purvis High School.

But how had Joan managed to get the girl's antibiotics? *Easy. She went to the school and took them from the clinic.*

Sandy sat there at that table, watching Joan go about making her something to eat. With Joan's back to her, Sandy's gaze darted around the room in search of anything she could use as a weapon. But nothing sat on the countertops save for a coffeepot, a blender, and a toaster.

Frustration and fear swirled inside her to drown out what little courage she'd mustered up in that basement. How was she going to get those keys from Joan, when the psycho carried a gun on her person? Sandy didn't know, but she had to try.

"Is it okay for me to go lie down?"

Joan glanced over her shoulder. "After you eat."

Sandy didn't want to eat. Her nerves were too bad to be able to hold anything down. On top of the terror gnawing at her insides, nausea now slithered through her as well.

But she would suffer through the sandwich if it would keep from angering Joan. "Okay."

Chapter Thirty-Six

Sandy somehow managed to choke down that turkey sandwich before Joan jerked her chin in the direction of the bedroom.

Shutting down her emotions, Sandy stood and made her way down the short hallway. She stepped inside the room, moved to the side of the bed, and slipped her robe free of her shoulders. It whispered down her body to pool at her feet.

Though Sandy couldn't see Joan's face, she could tell by the shift in her stance that she wasn't unaffected by Sandy's bold actions.

Sandy climbed onto the bed, gritting her teeth against the pain throbbing in her shoulder. "Will you lie down with me?"

"Why?"

Not wanting to overplay her hand, Sandy thought about all that Joan had inadvertently revealed to her. "My mother always brushed my hair when I was sick. It somehow made me feel better."

Joan simply stood there, looking at Sandy through the holes of that terrifying mask. And then she turned and left the room.

Sandy swallowed hard. Had she pushed the insane woman too far? Did Joan somehow know what she was up to?

Joan reappeared a moment later, holding a brush in her hand. "Roll over."

Sandy didn't want to roll over. Giving Joan her back put her in a very vulnerable position. And Sandy remembered the last time she'd lain splayed out on her stomach before that monster.

Determined to survive whatever Joan did to her, Sandy rolled to her stomach.

The bed dipped with Joan's weight, and the hesitant feel of the brush running through Sandy's hair caught her off guard.

"Like this?" Joan whispered, insecurity evident in her raspy voice.

Sandy's body was locked up tight from fear and anxiety, but she managed a soft, "Yes."

Joan brushed Sandy's hair for a good while, her fingers soon replacing the brush when she eventually crawled up closer and laid down next to her.

Neither of them spoke as Joan continued to touch and caress Sandy's head, until Joan finally broke the silence. "I've never had anyone brush my hair before."

Sandy stopped breathing. Was Joan silently asking for her hair to be brushed? If so, and Sandy managed to get that brush in her hand...

"I will brush it for you."

Joan's hand stilled against Sandy's head. She would either accept Sandy's offer or realize what she planned.

Moving to sit up, Joan slid to the edge of the bed, tension radiating from her thick enough so Sandy could feel it.

Sandy rolled over, her stomach knotted with so much anxiety she thought she'd be sick from it. She could see the brush in Joan's left hand, dangling from her fingers.

Sandy slowly sat up, her gaze locked on her potential weapon.

And then, psychopath did something that stunned Sandy to the point where she froze.

Joan laid the brush on top of the nightstand, pushed to her feet, and with her back to Sandy, began to remove the leather mask she wore.

Sandy's insides locked up with the thought of what she was about to do. Though she couldn't see Joan's face, she knew the woman's eyes would be wide and alert.

And then it hit Sandy like a ton of bricks. Joan was going to kill her. Which was the only reason she'd removed that mask.

Without facing Sandy, Joan suddenly rasped, "It's too risky to take you with me when I leave this place." She reached toward the pocket of her dress.

Horror struck, and Sandy's will to survive abruptly kicked in.

Gathering every ounce of strength she possessed, Sandy snatched up the hairbrush lying on that nightstand, reared up onto her knees, and brought the thick, wooden handle down as hard as she could against Joan's temple.

Joan cried out in surprise, her body lurching forward to stagger against the bathroom door, something clattering to the floor near her feet.

Sandy was on her in an instant. She slammed that brush into Joan's temple, again and again, until the maniac woman fell to her knees, her hair sliding free to reveal the shiny baldness of her head underneath.

A primal scream ripped from Sandy's throat. She dropped the brush she still held, locked her hands onto either side of Joan's bald head, and slammed her skull against the unforgiving wood of that floor.

Sandy wasn't sure how long she remained on Joan's back, beating her head on that floor when she realized the woman was no longer moving.

Sandy crawled off Joan, her entire body trembling from fear and adrenaline, and began going through the pockets of Joan's dress. She found nothing but a set of keys. No gun, no knife. And from the sound that had echoed throughout the room when Sandy had attacked, Joan had definitely dropped a knife.

Sandy's gaze swept the room, over the bed, the nightstand, and the open area in which Joan's body lay, but no weapons could be seen.

Flattening her body against the floor, Sandy searched under the bed but came up empty.

She stared numbly down at those keys in her hand, Joan's words skating through her mind. *"It's too risky to take you with me when I leave this place."* The crazy lunatic had definitely been about to kill her.

Jumping to her feet, Sandy donned her robe and hurried to the kitchen. She snatched open the first drawer she came to, only to find it empty.

Opening the second drawer, she discovered it bare as well. And on it went until Sandy had searched every drawer in that kitchen. Empty.

Why would Joan have no cooking or eating utensils? *Unless she'd already packed to leave.*

Not willing to waste any more time, Sandy clutched the set of keys she still held and turned in the direction of the basement. She would free the young girl chained up down there and get them both out of that place before Joan awoke in a rage.

Chapter Thirty-Seven

Sandy was trembling uncontrollably by the time she reached the basement door. She kept glancing over her shoulder, expecting Joan to be standing there, wearing her mask of horrors.

Opening the door, Sandy ran inside to find Selma lying on that bed, exactly as she'd left her.

"We have to hurry," Sandy gasped, rushing to the cuff around Selma's left wrist.

Sandy's hands shook so badly she dropped the keys three times before trying the first small one she came to.

It didn't work.

"Oh God," she cried, flipping past that key to try the next one. It slid into the cuff without issue.

With one of Selma's arms free, Sandy quickly moved to the next one, freeing it as well.

The cuffs at Selma's feet were opened next, sending the girl into a fit of near hysterical crying. "I thought you'd left me!"

"I told you I wouldn't leave you," Sandy rasped, grabbing hold of Selma's hand. "Now, we have to get out of here and fast!"

"Where is she?" Selma's voice came out in a terrified whisper.

"She's unconscious." Sandy ran for the open door, half dragging a naked Selma behind her. They raced up the stairs, stopping at the top to listen for signs that Joan could have awoken.

Met with silence, Sandy held a finger to her lips, signaling for Selma to stay quiet, and then led her as quickly as possible through the kitchen.

Glancing inside the bedroom, Sandy could see Joan's feet barely visible near the end of the bed.

Relief washed over her. They were going to make it.

Sandy arrived at the backdoor with a sobbing Selma in tow. She shushed the terrified girl once again and then flipped through the keys in search of one that she felt would fit. It didn't.

"Hurry!" Selma frantically gasped through her tears. "God, please hurry!"

Sandy flipped to the next key. "I'm trying!"

She wasn't sure how long she stood there, attempting to unlock that door, until she'd ran out of keys. "They don't work. None of them work!"

Spinning around, Sandy nearly ran into a hovering Selma. "We have to find the key to this door. It's on a keyring. I saw her with it earlier."

Without waiting to see if Selma followed, Sandy ran through the living room, taking a right at the hall instead of a left. She stopped and looked back at Selma. "Search the room on the right! There's a gun in this house also. If you find it, get it to me as fast as you can."

Selma shook her head, tears streaming down her face. "Don't leave me."

Anger surpassed Sandy's fear in that moment. She grabbed Selma by the shoulders and shook her. "If you don't do as I say, we are never getting out of here alive. Do you hear me? If she wakes up and finds us still in this house, she will kill us both. Now move!"

Something in Sandy's voice must have reached Selma's terrified brain. The trembling, naked girl ran past her toward the last room on the right.

Sandy proceeded down the hall, stopping in front of the first door on her left, only to find it locked.

Back to key hunting she went.

Finally locating the right key, she glanced down the hall to see that Selma had made it inside that room. Obviously that door hadn't been locked.

Sandy quickly stepped inside the room she stood in front of and flipped on the light. Her mouth opened in shock. There, covering most of the wall to her right, were dozens of newspaper clippings.

She stumbled forward, her gaze glued to images of the missing teens from Purvis High.

Louann Henderson, Maryann Jones, Destiny Murray, Heidi Birch, Mindy Reyes, Reginald Gilliam.

And then another article caught her eye, the newspaper clipping yellow and faded with age.

Sandy stepped in closer, squinting to read the barely legible text.

Reba Humphreys, a twenty-eight-year-old mother of two has been arrested for shooting her eight-year-old twins, Jonah and Joan Humphreys.

Sandy slapped a hand over her mouth. She couldn't have read that right.

Jonah Humphreys was pronounced dead at the scene, while his sister, Joan, remains in critical condition at Mercy General Hospital in Arkansas. Both children were shot with a 9mm handgun at point-blank range. Once in the head and twice in the stomach.

Sandy's hand pressed more firmly against her mouth in an effort to hold back the cry she felt rising there. Joan was Principal Humphreys.

Sandy thought about the scars she'd seen on Joan's stomach, the shaved head. Her mind then conjured up Principal Humphreys and the burn mark on the side of his face... The missing part of his ear.

Had that been the reason for Joan wearing the mask, so Sandy wouldn't recognize her as Jonah Humphreys?

They had been twins. Joan and Jonah. Only, Jonah had died from his injuries nearly thirty-four years ago, and Joan had been posing as her brother ever since.

Another faded newspaper article rested next to that one. Only this one wasn't faded and tattered. The headline read, *Reba Humphreys, Arkansas mother who shot eight-year-old twins, dies by lethal injection.*

The date of that clipping was only two years ago.

Around the same time the murders began in Montgomery, Sandy realized, continuing to read.

According to the article, Reba had shot both of her children after she'd begun dating an attorney at the firm where she worked.

He had broken things off with Reba shortly after discovering she had kids.

Reba Humphreys had gone insane, took the children for a ride, and then shot them both on a back road in the small town in Arkansas where she lived. She'd then shot herself in the arm, walked back to town, and reported her car hijacked.

Nothing about Reba's story lined up with her report. Her vehicle was discovered by a passerby later that same evening, the children still inside.

Reba's case had been heard by a jury of her peers, where she was found guilty of attempted murder, child endangerment, and the first-degree murder of her son, Jonah. She remained in prison for thirty-two years before she was put to death by the state of Arkansas.

Sandy staggered back a step, her mind unable to process everything she'd just read.

But it was true. The evidence of it stared back at her in the form of dozens of newspaper clippings.

She reached up and ripped one of the clippings from the wall, folded it up, and tucked it into the pocket of the robe she wore before getting back to the task at hand. Finding the keys to the front door.

She stumbled over to a desk perched along the far wall, noticing several dark-colored suits hanging on a rack next to it. Principal Humphreys' suits.

With a shudder, Sandy jerked open the long, narrow drawer in the front of the desk, nearly jumping back in horror when two pairs of handlebar mustaches came into view.

Joan had worn the mustaches to help camouflage her scars and to hide her identity.

Flicking the disgusting things aside, Sandy found what she sought. Keys.

Chapter Thirty-Eight

With the keyring in hand, Sandy hurried to the bedroom Selma had disappeared into to find the young girl wearing one of Joan's floral print dresses and bent over the nightstand drawer.

"Let's go," Sandy whispered, attempting to keep her voice down. "I found some keys."

She ran from the room with Selma tight on her heels.

"Did you find the gun?" Sandy asked, searching for a key she hoped would fit.

Selma whispered, "No," her voice impatient, fearful, and on the verge of panic. "Just please hurry!"

A moan echoed in the distance, telling Sandy without words that Joan was waking up.

"God, please hurry!" Selma was now clinging to Sandy's back with enough force she caused Sandy to drop the keys.

Tears of terror began to fill Sandy's eyes. She snatched up the keys with trembling hands and began randomly trying different ones in the locks.

"Sandyyyyy?" Joan screamed, the sound of her stumbling around in that room lending strength to Sandy's fear.

The lock suddenly freed.

Sandy twisted the knob in a frenzy, threw the door open, and shot out of that house as if the hounds of Hell were riding her back. And in a sense, she realized, they were.

Selma's breath punched in and out of her chest as she ran close behind Sandy. Neither of them slowed until they reached the locked gate in front of them.

Sandy wasn't about to hunt for a key to that lock. She climbed the chain link gate, throwing her leg over the barbed wire at the top.

It ripped into her legs, but she didn't slow.

"Hurry!" she hissed to Selma before dropping to the ground on the other side.

The young girl didn't hesitate. She followed Sandy over, crying out when the barbed wire tore into her flesh.

A shot suddenly rang out, exploding nearby to ricochet off the surrounding trees.

Selma jerked forward into Sandy's arms, a stunned look on her face.

"No, no. Noooo," Sandy breathed, hooking the young girl's arm around her neck and running for the tree line. "Move, Selma! You have to keep moving!"

Another shot rang out, sending a bullet to whiz through the bush next to Sandy's hip.

She ran faster.

* * * *

Sandy had no idea how long she'd been running through those woods, the young girl's weight continuously dragging her down and her bare feet in agony from stepping on briars and twigs.

But she wouldn't leave Selma behind, no matter how torn up her feet became. "Are you still with me?"

"Yes," Selma gasped in obvious pain. "Are we going the right way?"

Sandy had no idea, but she refused to voice the words aloud. She glanced behind her to see flames licking toward the sky. Joan had set the house on fire.

But Sandy needed Selma to hold on to even the smallest thread of hope, or she feared the young, terrified girl would give up. "Not much further."

They came to a stream surrounded by thick mounds of brush.

"Sannnnndy," Joan's singsong voice called out from somewhere in the distance.

Sandy had no idea how far away Joan truly was, but if she didn't hide Selma, and quick, she had no doubt they'd be found. After all, Joan knew those woods. Sandy didn't.

"I have to hide you," she whispered close to Selma's ear.

The young girl stumbled along beside her. "D-don't leave me out here."

"I'm not going to leave you. I'm going to lead her away from you."

Frantically glancing around, Sandy hobbled over to a patch of trees and lowered Selma's weight to the ground. She quickly grabbed up as much brush and leaves as she could find and covered the girl as best she could. "Don't move and do not make a sound."

Selma stared up at her through the visible cracks in the brush, her glittering eyes terrified in the faint light of the setting sun.

"I *will* come back for you. I promise." It would be dark soon, and Sandy had no idea which way would lead her out of their nightmare. She only knew which direction those flames came from, and that was back to Joan's house.

"Please don't leave me," Selma begged through her tears.

"I came back for you before, didn't I?"

Selma sniffled. "Y-yes."

"And I will return for you again. There is nothing in this world that would make me leave you out here. Now, stay as quiet as you can."

"Saaaaandy!" Joan's voice had definitely grown closer.

"I'll come back for you," Sandy whispered once more. And then, she ran.

Chapter Thirty-Nine

The moon rose higher in the starless sky the longer Sandy stumbled aimlessly through those woods.

She couldn't think beyond the agony of her mutilated feet, nor the sounds of Joan crashing through the brush not far behind her.

At least Joan hadn't found Selma.

Leaving the young girl behind, bleeding out in that brush, had been one of the most difficult things Sandy had ever done. But she'd had no choice. If they'd continued on at the snail's pace they'd been moving, they would both be dead by now.

The flames of Joan's burning house had long since disappeared from Sandy's view, telling her without words she'd walked a long distance.

A cramp caught Sandy's side, sending her doubling over in pain. She bit back a moan, slowing her steps to lean in an exhausted heap against a tree.

"I can hear you out there, Sandy. You can't escape me. There's nowhere to run to. We're miles from the nearest town."

Tears of fear and anger sprang to Sandy's eyes. She wasn't going to make it. Joan would find her and kill her while Selma lay hidden in that brush and died from blood loss and exposure.

The temperature had already begun to drop with the setting of the sun. And though Sandy's trek through the woods had kept her from freezing, Selma's still form would be a different story.

The last day Sandy had spent at school before she'd been abducted, the temperature outside had lowered to seventeen degrees. And if she had to guess, it was close to that once again.

For a girl wearing nothing but a thin dress and no shoes, Selma wouldn't last long without help.

"Saaaaandy."

Rage welled up inside Sandy to replace some of her fear. If she didn't do something to stop Joan, quick, she would never be able to keep her promise to Selma.

Scanning the ground near her bloodied feet, Sandy's gaze landed on a broken tree limb. It wasn't the best weapon of choice, but it was all she had available at the moment.

She lowered to her knees and, as quietly as possible, wrapped her fingers around the branch, lifted, and then slowly straightened.

"Sandy!" Joan snapped, obviously becoming angrier by the minute. "Come out right now, and I'll think about sparing your life."

Leaning her back firmly against the tree she stood next to, Sandy listened to Joan's footsteps growing ever closer. Which was no easy feat, considering her heart pounded so loudly in her ears it nearly drowned out her surroundings.

"You lied to me," Joan continued, her footsteps not ten feet away.

God, please help me, Sandy silently pleaded, gripping that limb in a tight hold and swinging out with everything she had.

It connected with Joan's head, knocking the lunatic off her feet.

Sandy swung again, bringing that heavy branch down hard against Joan's face.

The hot spray of blood splattered over Sandy's chest, letting her know she'd connected with Joan's nose.

Tossing the limb aside, Sandy scrambled around through the leaves until her fingers touched on the weapon Joan had dropped. The...gun.

Sandy snatched it up, attempting to hold it steady amidst the trembling of her hands.

She took aim at Joan's unconscious body and squeezed the trigger.

Nothing happened.

And why would it? Sandy had never shot a gun before. She had absolutely no idea how to use it.

With a cry of devastation, she dropped the weapon into the pocket of her robe, picked up that limb, and went to work on the monster's face.

She hit her repeatedly, blow after blow, until her exhausted arms could swing no more.

Dropping the limb onto Joan's hopefully dead body, Sandy scanned the trees. She had no idea in which direction she'd left Selma. And with the darkness now fully upon her, Sandy would never find her tonight.

With no other choice but to keep moving, Sandy stumbled forward, holding on to trees to keep upright. She would find help for Selma, even if she had to walk all night to do it.

Chapter Forty

Voices. Sandy could hear voices shouting from above her. "Call 911!"

"I did," a woman replied, sounding out of breath. "An ambulance is on the way. So are the police."

Was she dreaming? Sandy attempted to open her eyes, only to realize she lay on a hard surface, and the sun shone blindingly from above.

"She's waking up," a man pointed out in a hushed tone.

Sandy attempted to focus on his face, but the sun in her eyes prevented it. "W-where am I?"

"You're on County Road 18, ma'am. My wife and I found you here on our way to the store this morning."

Selma! It's morning, which means that Selma had been out there in those woods all night in the freezing temperatures.

Sandy moved to get up, only to realize the man's hands were on her shoulders. "Easy there. You're hurt. An ambulance is on the way."

Sandy's entire body hurt. Especially her feet. But none of that mattered. She had to get to Selma before she died. If she hadn't already. "T-there's a young girl still out there. Sh-she's been shot, and it's freezing. You have to — "

"Shhhhhh, don't try to get up. The police are on the way. You can tell them about the girl."

The faint sound of sirens could be heard in the distance, growing louder by the second.

Sandy turned her head in the direction of that blessed sound, only to notice a line of traffic parked along the side of the road.

She wondered how long she'd been lying there on that asphalt before being discovered. The fact that she hadn't been hit by a car was a miracle in itself.

A woman suddenly appeared, carrying a blanket in her arms. She covered Sandy's legs and then quickly backed up when the ambulance stopped nearby.

Sandy watched the medics descend the orange and white medical vehicle and hurry in her direction, with bags in hand.

They knelt on either side of her, opening their bags and questioning her as they withdrew several items. "Can you tell me your name?"

Sandy swallowed, shifting her gaze to the man who'd spoken. "Sandy. Sandy Patterson."

The medic's face paled. He glanced over at his partner and then peered down at Sandy once more. "You're safe now, Sandy. We're going to get you to the hospital. Can you tell me where you're hurt?"

Sandy opened her mouth to answer before licking her cracked and freezing lips to try again. "M-my baby…"

The medic peeled her covering back, his gaze scanning her body. "You have a baby with you?"

"I'm pregnant," Sandy rasped, the pain in her feet and shoulders beginning to filter into her psyche.

The medic replaced her blanket. "Try not to move. We'll do everything we can to help your baby."

Soon the police joined in the fray, questioning Sandy while the medics strapped her to a gurney and loaded her into the ambulance.

Sandy told the police about Selma, explaining that she'd left her wounded next to a creek beneath some brush.

She also informed them of the pistol resting in the pocket of her robe while filling them in as best she could about Joan and what had taken place in those woods.

The police retrieved the gun while calling for a chopper and the FBI to search for the injured teenager. "We'll find her, Mrs. Patterson. Try not to worry."

One of the officers joined Sandy in the back of the ambulance to continue questioning her on the ride to the hospital.

Sandy tried to stay alert, to answer the officer's questions as best she could. But her eyes slid shut against her will, and the darkness soon overtook her.

Chapter Forty-One

"Sandy? Sweetheart, can you hear me?"

Clark. The sound of her husband's voice brought Sandy's eyes open.

She lay in a warm bed. Bright lights shone from above her, telling her without words she'd made it to the hospital.

Twisting her head in the direction of that heavenly voice, Sandy stared into the eyes of the only man she'd ever loved, *would* ever love. "Oh, Clark. Are you really here?"

"I'm here, baby. And I'll never leave your side again." He took hold of her hand and brought it to his mouth.

Tears sparkled in his hazel-colored eyes. Sandy noticed dark circles rested beneath them.

"I thought I'd never see you again," she whispered, her own tears now surfacing.

Clark wiped at his face with the back of his hand. "I can't tell you what kind of Hell I've lived in for the past two weeks. I thought I'd lost you, Sandy. I thought you were—"

"My baby," Sandy gasped, her hand going to her abdomen.

Clark covered her hand with his. "The doctor says the baby is just fine, Sandy."

"You know about the baby?"

Nodding, Clark leaned in and brushed his lips across hers. "I found the pregnancy test in your car. God, Sandy, I can't tell you how relieved I am that you're okay. You're both okay."

But she wasn't okay, she quietly admitted to herself. And she wasn't sure she ever would be again.

"Selma!" she gasped, pulling back to search Clark's eyes.

"She's alive. They found her a few hours ago beneath a pile of brush and leaves. She was unconscious but alive."

Relieved beyond words, Sandy's eyes slid shut. "Is she going to make it?"

"According to her parents, the doctors are confident she'll make a full recovery."

Sandy smiled through her tears. "That's great news, Clark. I can only imagine how happy her parents are right now."

"They're outside in the hall, waiting for a chance to speak to you. Do you feel up to some company?"

"Why do they want to speak to me?" Sandy nervously asked.

Clark kissed the tip of her nose. "Because you saved their daughter's life. She would have died without you."

Giving Clark a nod, Sandy waited for him to raise her bed and move to open the door.

Murmurs of voices met her ears before a middle-aged couple entered the room.

The woman carried a vase of flowers in her hands, her eyes red rimmed from obvious crying.

"Hi, Sandy. My name is Patricia, and this is my husband, Robert. We're Selma's parents."

Moving deeper into the room, Patricia set the flowers on Sandy's bedside table and approached her side.

She took hold of Sandy's hand, tears suddenly falling from her eyes. "I don't know how to thank you for what you did for my baby. She's alive because of you."

Sandy allowed her own tears to fall. "She's one of the strongest people I've ever met. She kept going after she'd been injured, when even the strongest of men would have stopped."

"If you ever need us for anything," Robert announced, stepping in closer to his wife's side.

"Anything at all, please let us know. No matter how big or small. We will never be able to repay you for saving our Selma. But we'll do everything in our power to try."

Sandy found it hard to respond around the lump in her throat. "Thank you. Selma survived. That's all I care about."

Patricia leaned forward and touched Sandy's face before taking her husband's hand, nodding to Clark, and leaving the room.

"What about Joan?" Sandy asked Clark, once they were alone.

"The police found her in the woods, approximately a mile from where they located Selma."

Sandy's heart skipped a beat. "She's alive?"

A muscle ticked along Clark's jaw. "Let's not talk about her until you get better, okay?"

But Sandy wouldn't be deterred. "Where is she?"

Clark blew out an exhausted-sounding breath. "She's on the fifth floor."

Sandy began to tremble. Her mouth opened and closed several times before the words finally came. "She's in this hospital?"

"Easy, baby," Clark soothed, attempting to calm Sandy's movements. "She's cuffed to a hospital bed, and there's an officer standing guard outside her room. She can't hurt you. She'll never hurt you again."

Chapter Forty-Two

Sandy listened to the doctor explain that she would need to remain in the hospital for a couple days. Not only due to the shock, exhaustion, and malnutrition but because of the infection from the stab wound in her shoulder.

As much as she wanted to go home with Clark and put this chapter of her life behind her, Sandy also knew she would do what was best for her unborn baby.

A light tap sounded on the door to her hospital room. Clark lifted his brows as if to silently say, *I have no idea who that could be.* Sandy's parents had already spent the majority of the day with her, gushing over becoming grandparents, and had left to go home not half an hour ago.

Clark opened the door and then took a step back to admit a uniformed officer and two men wearing dark-blue suits into the room.

The officer thanked him and approached Sandy's bed. "Hi, Mrs. Patterson. My name is Officer Rayburn, and these two gentlemen are with the FBI."

Both men moved deeper into the room to stand near the foot of Sandy's bed.

The tallest of the two introduced the duo. "I'm SA Truman and this is SA Minton. We have a few questions we'd like to ask you, if you're feeling up to it."

Sandy sat up higher in bed. "Okay. I'll do my best."

Truman spoke first. "You mentioned that the woman who held you captive was known as Joan. Did you happen to learn a last name?"

Sandy gaped at the man. "You don't know?"

"Know what, ma'am?"

And then she remembered the house burning to the ground. Of course they wouldn't know. "Joan Humphreys. Her name is Joan Humphreys. She's been working at Purvis High School for the past ten years as Principal Jonah Humphreys."

Sandy went on to tell them about Reba, Jonah and Joan's mother, and the story she'd read in the newspaper clippings on the wall. "Reba died two years ago by lethal injection in Arkansas."

The two FBI agents glanced at each other.

"That was the trigger," Truman murmured, returning his attention to Sandy.

Sandy nodded toward a cabinet in the corner of her room. "The robe I was wearing when I escaped is in there. Check the pockets."

Clark retrieved the garment and felt inside both pockets. He pulled the folded newspaper clipping free and handed it to Truman.

The FBI agent unfolded the paper and read the article aloud. *"Reba Humphreys, a twenty-eight-year-old mother of two has been arrested for shooting her eight-year-old twins, Jonah and Joan Humphreys."*

He paused briefly before continuing.

"Jonah Humphreys was pronounced dead at the scene, while his sister, Joan, remains in critical condition at Mercy General Hospital in Arkansas. Both children were shot with a 9mm handgun at point-blank range. Once in the head and twice in the stomach."

"Jesus," Clark whispered, drawing everyone's attention to him. "No wonder the girl turned out to be a monster. What kind of a mother shoots her own children?"

Truman refolded the paper, his gaze still on Clark. "You'd be surprised at how many monsters are living among us, Mr. Patterson. And the numbers growing higher with every passing year."

"What will happen to Joan?" Sandy asked, a shudder passing through her.

"She'll be indicted and tried for the murders of Destiny Murray, Maryann Jones, Heidi Birch, and Louann Henderson."

Sandy blinked back the tears forming in her eyes. "What about Reginald Gilliam and Mindy Reyes?"

"Until their bodies are discovered," Truman answered in a quiet tone, "we can't charge her with their deaths."

Truman went on to question Sandy on everything she could remember about her time spent in Joan Humphreys' house of horrors, until Sandy could barely hold her eyes open another second.

She waited until the agents left and then drifted off to sleep, holding her husband's hand.

Epilogue

"Isn't she perfect?" Sandy whispered, watching her husband hold their newborn daughter in his arms.

Clark smiled without looking up, as if unable to take his gaze from the baby's face. "She is. And thank you for naming her after my mom."

"You don't have to thank me, Clark. I only wish that Molly were still alive to meet her in person."

Clark kissed his daughter's tiny forehead. "Mom would have loved her as much as I do."

"I shudder to think of what could have happened, Clark. It was a miracle of God that Molly survived my time spent in Joan's clutches."

Clark lifted his head, the torment Sandy had come to recognize shining in his eyes. "I know. It still keeps me awake at night. I think we need to homeschool Molly when she's old enough."

Sandy had given that a lot of thought as well. But had decided against it. "If we do that, then that monster wins. We can't allow her to dictate how we live our lives. Nor will I allow her to rent space inside my head for another minute. Molly will go to school, albeit a private school, with her peers. She will grow up to be smart, and we will teach her to be alert and strong."

Clark suddenly stiffened, his gaze lifting to the television playing softly across the room. "Turn that up."

Snatching up the remote, Sandy increased the volume, her mind instantly rebelling at what she saw on the screen.

Joan sat in a courtroom, her short hair spiked on top, accenting the scar on her cheek and the missing part of her ear. She faced forward, her chin held high and a smirk on her terrifying face.

She'd been found not guilty by reason of insanity and was sentenced to spend the rest of her days in a mental institution, where she would be locked away from society and could get the proper medication and care.

Sandy stared in stunned disbelief at Joan's face, her mind unable to comprehend that Joan wouldn't spend a single day behind the bars of a prison.

"What the...?" Sandy heard Clark breathe, apparently in as much shock as she was.

And then, the screen changed to an image of a young brunette girl standing next to an equally dark-haired little boy. Both children had huge smiles on their faces.

It took a moment for Sandy to realize that the children in the image were Joan and her twin brother, Jonah.

The screen changed once more, this time to show an eight-year old Joan lying in a hospital bed with her head shaved and tubes coming from her mouth and nose.

Something shifted inside Sandy as she watched Joan's story through a haze of tears. Joan had been a product of her mother's making. She'd never stood a chance. Perhaps if her twin brother had survived, things might have been different for Joan. But he hadn't.

Joan had grown up to become a serial killer, a monster who preyed on innocent, young girls who represented everything she would never be.

As for Reggie and Mindy Reyes, their bodies had yet to be found, but the FBI were still searching and felt confident they would find them somewhere on the three-hundred-acre tract of land that Joan had been leasing for the past ten years.

Another screen change produced an old newspaper clipping similar to the ones that Sandy had discovered on the wall of Joan's bedroom.

In the clipping was a picture of a medium-size sedan parked along what looked to be a dirt road. Both back doors stood open to reveal an enormous amount of blood on the back seat. Jonah's and Joan's blood.

Sandy found it too difficult to wrap her mind around what had taken place on that September day thirty-four years in the past. When Reba Humphreys had taken the life of her only son for the love of a man she couldn't have. And she'd shot her daughter in the head and stomach, leaving Joan unable to bear children.

Had Joan not survived, five teenagers in Alabama would not be dead today.

Sandy tuned out the monotone voice of the channel seven news anchorwoman and slowly raised her gaze to the top of that old, faded newspaper clipping. There, in the bold, black letters of a thirty-four-year-old newspaper article: *The girl who lived to tell...*

Thank you for reading The Girl Who Lived to Tell!

If you enjoyed this story, read below for a sneak peek into the pages of The Silencer: a gripping psychological thriller.

As with this book, The Silencer contains triggers of physical abuse, sexual trafficking, and torture. Read with caution.

I ask that if you are gracious enough to leave a review to please not leave spoilers that would potentially ruin the experience of other readers.

Another book you might enjoy is, I Am Elle: a chilling psychological thriller. Book one in the Elle Series is about a young girl who endures the most heinous acts imaginable and survives.

Chapter One

Oliver Quick rubbed at his bloodshot eyes and glanced at the blinking phone on his desk.

He wondered how long the caller would hold before growing impatient and hanging up altogether.

The door to his office abruptly opened and his secretary, Joyce Meeks, poked her head inside.

She stared at him with a disapproving look before marching across the room to snatch up the phone. "I apologize for the wait, Mr. Williams. Oliver is on another line. I'd be happy to take a message if you'd rather not continue to hold."

Oliver listened to Joyce repeat his brother-in-law, Aaron Williams's, words back to him, understanding full well she did it for his own benefit.

Joyce Meeks had been with Oliver since he'd opened Quick Investigations a little more than five years ago. Though she spoke with the voice of a seasoned general and wore her hair in a similar fashion, she had kind blue eyes. And she thought of Oliver as the son she never had.

She returned the phone receiver to its home with a little more force than was probably necessary and pierced Oliver with an accessing stare. "Too much scotch last night?"

Oliver leaned back in his chair, propping his feet on the corner of his desk, and ignored Joyce's reference to his late-night drinking. "What did Aaron want?"

"Besides calling to invite you to the children's birthday party next weekend? I have no idea. Why don't you call him back and find out?"

Oliver inwardly cringed. Spending his weekend with a bunch of screaming kids didn't bode well with his hangover.

He opened his mouth to announce that very thing, when the trill of the phone once again echoed from his desk, sending an unwelcome pain shooting through his skull.

"Serves you right," Joyce snapped, striding toward the open door. "That drinking is going to be the death of you." The door clicked shut behind her.

"Quick Investigations," Oliver nearly growled, answering the incoming call.

A brief pause ensued. "Hello, Oliver, it's Richard Holland."

Oliver's stomach tightened. There would be only one reason the supervisor of the FBI field office in Huntsville, Alabama would be calling him. They needed his help.

"SSA Holland," Quick acknowledged. "It's been a minute." *Nearly six years to be exact.*

Richard cleared his throat. "That it has. Look, Quick, I could use your help."

"My help? With what?" But Oliver knew. He'd already heard about the dismembered body discovered under the pier in Panama City Beach. It was all over the news. "I'm not a profiler any longer, Richard. I haven't been for years."

"A profiler isn't something you do, Quick. It's who you are."

Oliver refrained from pointing out the obvious. The last serial killer he'd profiled had not only killed Oliver's wife, he'd gone on to kill six more women shortly afterward.

"I'm headed to Panama City Beach," Richard continued without preamble. "Can you meet me for lunch?"

The last thing Oliver needed was the smell of greasy food invading his hungover, consistently throbbing head. But the profiler in him couldn't resist meeting with the leader of the Behavioral Analysis Unit in Huntsville. "Salty Sue's in half an hour."

"I'll be there." The line went dead.

Oliver replaced the phone receiver and stood. He wandered over to his large office window to stare out at the busy Destin traffic of Back Beach Road.

His hands sank into the pockets of his navy-blue slacks. He watched the cars move bumper-to-bumper in an impatient line of horn-blowing maniacs.

April had loved this place, Oliver thought, his gaze moving to the beach beyond. She'd wanted to raise their children there...children they would never have.

The old, familiar ache that always began in his heart with thoughts of April traveled through his chest to settle in his gut.

Nausea was instant.

Oliver locked his teeth together, his eyes sliding closed to shut out the view before him.

He groaned deep in his throat, allowing the memories of his beautiful April to wash through him.

Her laughter, the always present twinkle in her pretty green eyes, and the dimple in her cheek when she smiled flashed behind his closed lids with haunting clarity.

His mind instantly rebelled against what he knew would come next, but he could no longer block it out than he could stop the waves from crashing onto the shore of the beach in front of him.

April lying in that morgue. A perfectly straight incision on her bruised and battered throat. Her larynx had been removed with the precision of a surgeon and then the wound sewn closed.

Oliver shuddered, unable to push the images from his mind. His wife, his precious April had been repeatedly raped, violated in the vilest of ways. Her breasts had been burned in numerous places, along with her genitals.

She'd been bound for days, unable to speak or scream while her killer endlessly tortured her to death. He'd then painted her fingernails and toenails a blood-red color...postmortem.

April had been his sixth victim in less than a month, categorizing him as a serial killer. He'd been dubbed *the Silencer* by the media for removing his victim's voice boxes days before he ended their lives. And then he'd painted their fingernails and toenails. Always with the same red color.

"Oliver?"

Somewhere in the far recesses of his mind, Oliver knew Joyce spoke to him, but he couldn't seem to pull back from the grief swimming inside him. He hadn't caught April's killer. His profile had been off.

The Silencer had vanished almost six years ago, leaving no evidence to his identity behind.

Oliver had worked day and night to profile the sicko, only to come up empty. He'd been too close to the case, making him less than objective.

His emotions, grief and helpless rage over the loss of his wife, had stood between him and his ability to be openminded and detached.

The Silencer had slipped through his fingers.

A hand rested against Quick's back, and his secretary's voice finally penetrated his guilt-filled mind. "Oliver, are you all right?"

He swallowed with more than a little difficulty. "I'm fine, Joyce. Thank you."

"There's a man here to see you."

He answered without turning away from the window. "Have him make an appointment. I'm meeting someone in ten minutes for lunch."

"But—"

"Please, Joyce. I can't do this right now."

Something in his voice must have clued her in to his current mental status. Her hand fell away, and the sound of her shoes slapping on the tile floor could be heard over the horns blowing from the streets beyond.

Oliver waited until the door closed behind her, then trailed to his desk, plucked up his suit jacket, and left by way of the back.

Chapter Two

Richard Holland waited until the waitress moved away before extending his hand across the table to Oliver. "Thank you for coming on such short notice."

Oliver accepted the man's outstretched palm and took a seat. "It's good to see you, Richard. So, tell me what you've got."

Holland nodded, pushing a yellow folder toward Oliver. "You always did get right to the point."

Opening the folder, Oliver took in the sight before him.

Dozens of photos were inside; images of the dismembered body of the female found beneath the pier in Panama City Beach.

Oliver hardened himself against his emotions. "I understand the heinousness of the crime, but why has the FBI been called in on this?"

Richard set his water glass down and wiped his mouth with a cloth napkin. "Because there were two similar cases last month less than an hour from here over the Alabama line. The Baldwin County Sheriff's Office called us in to assist."

Oliver's jaw tightened. "Similar cases?"

"There's enough similarities for us to ascertain it's the same guy."

"A serial killer," Oliver stated in a deadly soft tone.

Richard nodded. "The Bay County Police Department notified us of the body found beneath the pier. They called in the local sheriff's department and the FBI to help with the investigation. My team is there now."

April's cold, pale body flashed behind Oliver's eyes. "Why are you coming to me with this? You have an efficient team working with you in Huntsville and a dozen more at your disposal at the Quantico office."

"Because you're one of the best profilers I've ever known, and I'd like your help with this."

Oliver closed the folder and got to his feet. "I'm a private investigator now. I no longer hunt serial killers, Richard. I haven't since—"

"Since April died," Richard interrupted, catching Oliver off guard.

"I understand your reluctance, Quick." Richard leaned across the table and flipped the folder back open. "But this woman had a family, a husband...and a child on the way. She can't tell us who did this to her, but I'm willing to bet that you can."

Richard lifted a picture of the woman's decapitated head and held it up for Oliver to see. "Her husband needs closure. As do her parents."

Oliver stared down into the lifeless eyes of the woman in the picture for long moments. She'd been pregnant…just as April had.

Swallowing back the bile that rose in his throat, Oliver tore his gaze from the sickening photo and returned to his seat.

As badly as he wanted to, he simply couldn't bring himself to walk away. "What's the victim's name?"

"Clayton. Jennifer Clayton."

Oliver let that sink in. "I'll need to see the scene where the body was found."

Richard placed the picture back in the folder and tucked it inside his briefcase. "I'll take you there right after you get some food in you. From the look of your eyes, you could use it."

Oliver wasn't hungry, but he would order anyway. He needed something to soak up the overabundance of alcohol from the night before. And he needed strength for what he knew lay ahead.

* * * *

After driving to his condo to change into jeans and running shoes, Oliver donned his Oakley's and followed Holland to the normally busy beach in Panama City.

The expected yellow tape and police presence surrounded the massive pier to keep onlookers from contaminating what was left of the crime scene.

The rising tide from the previous two nights had no doubt destroyed what evidence had been left behind. Which Oliver doubted would be any.

But it wasn't evidence Oliver looked for. Most serial killers were meticulous. They didn't leave behind incriminating evidence. No, he needed to see what the killer saw, hear what he heard...and figure out why he chose that particular place to dispose of the body.

Oliver trailed along behind Holland, his gaze touching on everything around him. From the mobs of curious onlookers to the surrounding storefronts and restaurants in close proximity to the pier.

His gaze then swung to the dunes behind him, coming to rest on the taped-off markings embedded in the sand. *Drag marks, most likely from a body.*

How had the killer dragged a bag of body parts down to the pier without being noticed by anyone?

The crowd of people gathered around, attempted to move in closer, forcing the police to order them back.

Though it had been two days since Jennifer Clayton's body had been discovered, the onlookers hadn't seemed to grow bored with the taped-off crime scene.

As if reading Oliver's thoughts, Richard stepped in closer to his side. "It's going to be like this for a while longer, I'm sure. With so much sand and the size of that pier, God knows how long it'll take them to finish processing the scene."

A middle-aged officer keeping the crowds back turned as Holland and Oliver approached the tape.

Holland produced his credentials, spoke a few words to the officer while jerking his chin in Oliver's direction.

Oliver nodded to the officer, ducking beneath the yellow tape the officer lifted for him and then held up a hand, indicating he wanted to go down alone.

Holland didn't attempt to follow, nor did Oliver expect him to. He'd worked with the man long enough in the past to know that Richard understood his particular profiling methods.

Oliver didn't bother to search the sugary white beach sand around the pier. He wouldn't find anything there. Besides, the local police department was still crawling through the scene with the precision of ants erecting a mound.

With so much sand in the vicinity, they were forced to sift through it, inch by inch.

Shutting out everything around him, Oliver's mind slipped into profiler mode. His vision grew tunneled and his senses became heightened. Sounds from the crashing waves of the Gulf faded to the background, along with the murmuring of voices surrounding the crime scene.

The bright noonday sun turned into a silvery moon in Oliver's mind, casting shadows along the dunes and sending the long, giant pier plummeting into darkness.

Oliver's head swiveled to the right as he imagined the lights along the rails of the pier coming on at sunset.

His gaze traveled to the local restaurant sitting a short distance up the beach. Music spilled out from the open deck to be swept away on the warm moonlit breeze.

The lights shone brightly through the fog hovering over the Gulf, illuminating the dunes between the deck of the restaurant and the pier.

Smiling faces of tourists moved through his mind, their laughter and friendly banter growing in volume in order to be heard over the music thumping in the background.

No one from that deck would likely notice a lone figure making their way beneath the pier.

His gaze swept to the left, to a souvenir shop that probably closed their doors at five o'clock sharp on the weekdays. No danger of being seen from there.

On it went, with Oliver studying his surroundings, an imaginary garbage bag in his hand growing heavier with each passing second.

He imagined himself pulling into the parking lot up the hill, waiting for his opportunity to move.

But why the busy pier area? There are literally hundreds of miles of beachfront to dump a body. Yet he chose this particular spot. Why…?

Because he's a narcissist. Torture isn't enough for him. He garners some kind of rush from the threat of exposure. He believes the women are beneath him. He thinks himself superior…

The face of the decapitated woman appeared in Oliver's mind, pulling him back from the abyss, back to the dozens of eyes watching him expectantly.

He sought out Holland, who promptly moved to his side.

"What are you thinking, Quick?"

Oliver held the shorter man's gaze. "I'd need to see the autopsy results to be sure, but I'm willing to bet that the unsub drowned the victim before cutting her up."

"What makes you think that?"

Oliver shrugged. "He's grandstanding by bringing her out here and leaving her to be found. But the water, the water is significant to him somehow."

"Then why cut her up?"

"I don't know yet," Oliver stated in a matter-of-fact tone. "But I'd like to see the body now."

"Okay. Let's go."

Oliver strode along next to Holland, his mind still mulling over the surrounding establishments. "Are there any cameras on the restaurant and souvenir shop?"

Richard shook his head. "Some of the shops down the beach have cameras, but the ones closest to the pier don't."

"I'm betting he knew that," Oliver admitted with near certainty. "He's been in both places. More than once."

Holland's gaze narrowed. "He cased the places before he chose this spot."

"Exactly."

They reached the parking area at the top of the hill. Holland hesitated before opening his car door. "I'll have the receipts pulled at both places for the last month. Hopefully we get a hit on something."

Oliver nodded, fishing his keys out of the pocket of his jeans. "I'd like to question the staff myself. Once I've seen the body."

Richard slid behind the wheel of his vehicle. "Follow me."

Chapter Three

Oliver arrived at the medical examiner's office behind Holland twenty minutes later.

The two men entered the building, side by side, making their way to the back where the refrigerated bodies were held.

It had been years since Oliver had darkened the door of the place.

Not much had changed, he noted, recognizing the familiar scent of the chemicals used in the back. It was a smell he would know anywhere. A smell he associated with…death.

A pretty brunette exited the lady's room on the left, nearly running into Quick in the process.

She barely flinched. "Excuse me, gentlemen, may I help you?"

Oliver pushed his Oakley's to the top of his head.

He swiftly took in her appearance, noting her air of confidence and the direct look she gave him without breaking eye contact.

She was no doubt used to dealing with his type. And by his type, he meant suits. Even though he wore jeans at the moment.

Richard produced his credentials. "We're with the FBI. We need to see the body of the dismembered female that was recently brought in."

The brunette eyed his identification. "I'm assuming you've been here before and know your way around."

"We have," Richard assured her, returning his ID to his pocket.

She simply nodded before skirting them both, the clicking of her heels echoing off the hallway walls as she strode away.

Richard ambled ahead, stopping outside the door that read, *Medical Examiner*.

He rapped on it once with his knuckles and then turned the knob, entering the chilled room without further notice.

Oliver trailed in behind him, blocking out the smells invading his senses.

A man Oliver hadn't met before stood over a stainless-steel table, the florescent lights above him reflecting off his partially bald head. His gloved hands hovered above the corpse of a man that appeared to be in his late fifties.

The tag on the doctor's coat pocket read, *Dr. T. Ramsey.*

Ramsey peered up over the rim of his glasses, glancing at Oliver and then Richard. "Holland. I figured you'd be down here before long."

"Hello, Teddy," Holland greeted, approaching the table. "Have you met my associate, Oliver Quick?"

The doctor shook his head, meeting Oliver's gaze. "I haven't had the pleasure, but I've certainly heard of you. Your reputation as a profiler is remarkable."

Oliver brushed the compliment aside, uncomfortable with the praise. As was his way, he got right to the point. "Has Jennifer Clayton's body been autopsied?"

Ramsey sent him a quick nod. "It has. She was top priority." He jerked his chin toward the refrigerated drawers along the opposite wall. "She's in number eighteen."

"Thank you, Doctor." Oliver trailed across the room, pulling open the designated drawer.

The chilly air of the refrigeration sent goosebumps peppering his arms.

He stared down at the black body bag, remembering back to when he'd had to identify April.

His heart began to pound, dread and nausea growing stronger by the second.

"Is everything all right?"

The sound of Richard's voice broke into his anxiety.

With a surprisingly steady hand, Oliver took hold of the body bag's zipper and slowly glided it down. He stopped when Jennifer's head came into view.

The sight of a corpse always unsettled him. But the murdered ones... The murdered ones were the worst. The frozen terror in their eyes, as if they took those last horrendous moments with them to eternity.

Doctor Ramsey appeared on the opposite side of the drawer, holding a folder in his hands.

Oliver raised his gaze to the doctor's. "What was the cause of death?"

"Drowning. Repeatedly."

Surely Oliver hadn't heard him right. "I'm sorry, did you say repeatedly?"

Ramsey opened the folder and pulled a paper free. He handed it to Oliver. "Those were my findings. She'd been drowned more than once, resuscitated only to be drowned again. It's hard to tell the exact number of times this was done to her. I can only assure you that it's what killed her."

Oliver glanced down into the woman's milky-colored eyes and then met the doctor's gaze once more. "So, he cut the body up postmortem." It wasn't a question.

"Most of the body," the doctor muttered, unzipping the bag the rest of the way. He reached inside and lifted a pale-colored hand up for Oliver's perusal. The ring finger was missing. "The fourth finger was removed before her death, as was the fetus she carried."

Oliver digested that bit of information, swallowing back the bile that rose in his throat. Jennifer Clayton's unborn child had been removed from her body before her death.

Unclenching his teeth enough to speak, Oliver asked, "Was the baby vaginally removed or..."

The doctor shook his head. "He was cut from the abdomen and then the wound sewn closed."

"He..." Oliver began.

"The gender of the fetus was discovered from the victim's medical records," Dr. Ramsey offered, saving Oliver the task of asking the dreaded question aloud.

Getting a grip on his emotions, Oliver shut them down completely. "I take it the fetus wasn't recovered?"

"No, I'm afraid not," Ramsey answered.

Oliver let that sink in. "How far along was Mrs. Clayton in her pregnancy?"

Doctor Ramsey's gaze softened. "Thirty-two weeks."

Oliver briefly glanced at Holland. "That's four deaths he's responsible for. Not three."

Without waiting for a response from Richard, Oliver nailed the doctor with another question. "Was a wedding ring recovered?"

Richard answered for the doctor. "Nothing has been recovered. Not her clothes, jewelry, or her car."

Pinching the bridge of his nose, Oliver questioned the doctor further. "Was there any evidence of rape, strangulation, any ligature marks or other wounds besides the obvious?"

The doctor nodded. "There were ligature marks on her wrists, consistent with rope. We also found some marks and residue on her lower face, telling us that her mouth had been duct taped for quite some time. I found no evidence of rape."

That surprised Oliver. According to Richard, both the women discovered in Alabama had been raped. "How long was Mrs. Clayton missing before her body was found?"

"A week," Richard answered quietly.

Oliver's detachment momentarily slipped. Jennifer Clayton had been tortured, drowned, and resuscitated, only to be tortured again and again before the killer grew tired and drowned her a final time. But not before he cut her unborn child from her body.

"He tortured her for a week." Oliver took a step back and met Holland's gaze. "That's almost unheard of, Richard. Most serial killers don't last beyond three days before their rage drives them to kill."

When Holland simply stood there, silently watching him, Oliver asked, "Was the MO the same with the Alabama victims?"

Richard nodded his confirmation. "Aside from the fact they'd been raped, both victims were found along the shore of the Gulf in Alabama, their dismembered bodies stuffed into garbage bags and tied to a dock."

Oliver knew the answer to his next question, but he asked it anyway. "Private or public docks?"

"Public. Why?"

"It's the epilogue to his fantasy." Oliver glanced between Holland and Ramsey. "His last show of humiliation before he moves beyond them in search of a new vic."

A deep indention appeared between Ramsey's eyes. "And the finger he removes?"

Oliver returned his attention to the woman's hand, the doctor still held. "Since it's customary to wear a wedding ring on that particular finger, my guess is it's significant to him somehow. A cheating wife or girlfriend."

Ramsey placed the hand back inside the body bag and zipped it up. "Are you saying he removes the finger as a form of punishment?"

Oliver shrugged. "Partly. But it's definitely his signature. And he's most likely keeping the wedding rings as trophies."

"But why the babies?" Richard asked. "Why take pregnant women?"

Oliver swung his gaze in Richard's direction. "Were the other fetuses removed in the same manner as Jennifer Clayton's?"

Richard slightly shook his head. "According to the reports, the unborn children hadn't been removed."

"Then why was Jennifer's?" Oliver peered down at the now zipped bag containing

Jennifer's body, watching as Dr. Ramsey slowly eased her drawer back into its refrigeration unit.

Oliver spun on his heel and headed toward the door without a word to either of the men behind him.

"Quick?" Richard caught up with Oliver as he stepped into the hall. "What are you thinking?"

Oliver didn't slow. "I need to see the reports from the two vics in Alabama."

"I can get them to you within the hour, but you haven't answered my question."

Sailing out the double doors to the parking lot beyond, Oliver dug out his car keys and paused next to his vehicle. "The killer saw something in Jennifer Clayton, something he didn't see in the others."

Oliver unlocked his door and pulled it open. "He removed her unborn child from her body."

"Plus, Jennifer Clayton hadn't been raped," Richard unnecessarily pointed out."

"Yeah," Oliver muttered softly, more to himself than for Richard's benefit. "And I need to know what changed for him with Jennifer. Something changed." With that, he slid behind the wheel, cranked the stifling hot SUV, and backed out of the parking lot.

Chapter Four

Oliver sat on his couch later that evening, drink and folder in hand. He couldn't get Jennifer Clayton out of his mind.

She'd had her unborn child removed from her body before her death. *Why?*

Mrs. Clayton had been a twenty-eight-year-old preschool teacher with her whole life ahead of her...her hopes and dreams snuffed out by a sadistic monster bent on pain and humiliation.

Opening the folder, Oliver scanned the details of the first page until he found what he looked for... Jennifer's husband, Mark Clayton.

Mark was a sales rep for a local pest control company in town. He was thirty-two years old, just four years older than his deceased wife.

Oliver made a mental note to visit Mr. Clayton first thing the following morning.

He laid the folder aside and picked up the next one. Inside were images and details of one of the women found in Alabama. Blonde hair, blue eyes, twenty-seven years of age.

Laying that folder aside, Oliver opened the next one only to find similarities to the other two victims. Same hair and eye color.

He glanced at the woman's age, not surprised to find she'd been under thirty at the time of her death as well.

The victims aren't random. They're surrogates.

Oliver took another swig of his scotch, glancing at the clock on the wall. It was closing in on ten pm.

He set his drink on the coffee table, along with the folders he held, and then snatched up his cell phone and put in a call to his secretary, Joyce.

She answered on the third ring. "Hello?"

"Hi, Joyce. I'm not going to be in the office the rest of the week. Will you call my sister and let her know that I won't be making the birthday party tomorrow?"

"Is everything all right?" Though she sounded sleepy, concern lined the edges of her voice.

Oliver chose his words carefully. "Everything is fine, Joyce. I've been asked to profile for the BAU on a local case."

"The BAU? I thought you were done working with them."

"It's only temporary, I promise. I'd like for you to keep the office open in my absence."

His secretary remained quiet for a moment. "It's obviously something serious if they need a profiler. Should I be concerned?"

Since she wasn't a young blonde, Oliver knew she had nothing to worry about.

He attempted to put her mind at ease. "Not at all, Joyce. Hopefully, we'll have everything wrapped up quickly, and I'll be back in the office before you know it."

A brief pause ensued. "Okay. I'll call Mindy and let her know you can't make the party. If you need my help with anything, just let me know."

"Thank you, Joyce. Just knowing you're taking care of the office is more help than anything. Have a good night."

He hung up the phone and placed it on the coffee table next to the folders before downing the rest of his scotch.

The doorbell rang, eliciting an annoyed growl in the back of his throat.

He surged to his feet and marched across the room.

A look through the peephole conjured up Jason Haney's face.

Oliver opened the door and stepped back to allow his lifelong friend's entrance. "You're out kind of late."

Jason sauntered into the room and made his way to the bar to pour himself a drink. "It's only ten fifteen. Can I get you a refill?"

Oliver handed him his empty glass and followed him to the bar.

"What are you up to this evening?" Jason quickly poured them two drinks.

Oliver waited for Jason to pass him his scotch and then took a deep swallow. "I'm actually working."

"At this hour?"

Oliver rubbed at the back of his neck. "I've been asked to assist the FBI on a case."

With his glass to his lips, Jason turned to face Oliver, his eyebrows nearly in his hairline. "No kidding?"

Oliver returned to his position on the couch and waited for Jason to take a seat across from him in the recliner. "I was a bit surprised, myself. I mean it's been years."

Jason sat forward with his elbows resting on his jean-clad knees, swirling the dark liquid around in his scotch glass. "You're profiling again?"

Oliver shrugged. "Not on a permanent basis. I'm merely assisting them on a local case."

Understanding registered in Jason's brown eyes. "Ah. The girl that was found under the pier in Panama City Beach."

"Yes," Oliver admitted before taking a drink of his scotch. "Two more were killed earlier in the month over the Alabama line. Same MO."

Jason stared back at him without blinking. "A serial killer. Are you going to be able to handle this?"

Oliver understood Jason's concern. He'd watched Oliver fall apart after April's death and had been by his side through the frustration and rage of letting her killer slip through his fingers. "I can handle it."

But he wasn't so sure he believed his own words.

Jason continued to stare, his dark-brown eyes brimming with concern.

"I said I can handle it," Oliver bit out, more annoyed with himself than with Jason.

"Okay then." Jason sighed. "I'll let it drop. Just know that I'm here if you need to talk." He finished off his drink, set the empty glass on the coffee table, and pushed to his feet. "I have to go. I'm meeting someone at Gulfscape in half an hour."

Oliver stood as well. "You have a date at eleven o'clock?"

Jason grinned. "Jealous?"

"Not at all. I'm perfectly content sleeping alone. But you go and have a good time. I'll just live vicariously through you."

Jason sobered. "It's been almost six years, Quick. Don't you think it's about time you lived a little?"

Oliver knew his friend spoke the truth, but he couldn't bring himself to enter the dating scene. Not yet. "I'm far too screwed up to attempt dating. My emotional baggage alone is enough to outweigh the best of intentions."

With an understanding nod, Jason made his way to the door and pulled it open. He stopped on the porch of Oliver's beachside condo, appearing to consider his next words. "We all miss her, my friend. She was a heck of a lady. A lady that would want you to go on living. Even if it means without her."

Jason trailed off the porch and sauntered over to his Harley parked next to Oliver's black SUV.

He plucked up his helmet and threw his leg over the bike. "Think about what I said."

Oliver merely nodded. "Since when did you start wearing a helmet?"

"Since I let my insurance lapse. You know how Florida laws are. If you don't carry insurance, you have to cover the bean."

Oliver grinned, watching Jason pull the helmet over his shaggy blond hair.

"Give it hell," Oliver called out before closing the door. He blew out an exhausted breath, grabbed up the empty glasses, and carried them to the sink at the bar.

Memories of April's smiling face bombarded him as he grabbed a sponge, turned on the water, and absently began to wash out the glass he held.

"You really should get the black leather sofa, Oliver. It suits your sexy, profiling self."

Her husky laughter swirled through his mind, bringing with it nearly unbearable pain.

The sound of glass shattering brought Oliver out of his musings. He'd been so caught up in his memories, he hadn't realized how much pressure he'd applied to the glass.

He dropped the sponge, his gaze now fixated on the steady stream of blood washing down the drain.

He'd cut his hand.

Deep.

Below are two chapters of I Am Elle for those curious about the tone of the Elle Trilogy.

Prologue

Wexler, Alabama

Population 2415

"Elle!" Elijah Griffin shouted, the back door slamming in the distance, a testament to his mood.

He'd been drinking again.

Elenore hovered behind the chicken coop, her bare feet catching on briars in her haste to escape her father.

"Elle Griffin? So help me God, girl, I will take my belt to you if you don't bring your butt here at once!"

She didn't want to leave the safety the shadows of the chicken coop provided. But she was afraid not to.

If she remained there, and her father found her hiding from him, he would hurt her. Badly.

Tears gathered in her eyes, but she blinked them back. One thing Elijah Griffin hated worse than disobedience was tears.

Elenore wiped at her eyes with the hem of her dress and stepped from behind the coop.

The evening sun had begun its descent, casting shadows along the side of the house and hiding her father's expression from view.

But Elenore didn't need to see his face to understand what he wanted from her, what he'd been taking from her for years.

She lowered her head and slowly moved in his direction.

"Where've you been, girl?" He gripped her upper arm in a painful hold. "Get your butt in that house."

Elenore stumbled toward the steps at the back door. She swallowed back the panic that rose in her throat at the knowledge of the horror that awaited her inside.

She could feel her father tight on her heels, knew he would be on her within seconds.

But hard as she tried, Elenore could fight the tears no longer.

And the tears would make it worse...so much worse.

"Are you crying?" he slurred, his hand suddenly in her hair.

He jerked her around to face him. "What have I told you about crybabies?"

"I-I won't do it again."

He stared at her for achingly long moments, unsteady on his feet. "Get in your room."

Elenore didn't want to go into her room. She knew what would happen to her once inside.

He backhanded her across the face.

The copper taste of blood filled her mouth.

With her jaw now throbbing to the beat of her heart, Elenore staggered toward her bedroom door, Elijah following close behind.

She could hear the buckle of his belt tinkering as he released it and slid it free of his beltloops. She turned to face him.

"Take it off," he demanded, nodding to her dress.

Her fingers trembled so badly they barely functioned.

He took a step toward her. "Now!"

Elenore jumped, lifting her shaky fingers to the first button at the top of her dress.

There would be no stopping her father from what he intended to do to her. There never was.

Elenore took a slow, deep breath, lifting her gaze to a place just beyond his shoulder. She forced her eyes to relax until the wall behind him faded into the distance. Her vision grew tunneled, and her mind floated off to a place where nothing or no one could touch her. Especially not her father...

Chapter One

Ten Years Later

Elenore kept her gaze on the floor and accepted the two bags of groceries the bag boy handed her.

"Do you need some help carrying them to your car?"

She knew the bag boy spoke to her, but she pretended not to hear him. Besides, if he saw that she didn't have a car, there would be no hiding the pity that would surely come.

And Elenore hated pity, nearly as much as she despised her father's pet name for her. *Elle.* It wasn't so much the name itself as the way he said it...like a caress. She inwardly shuddered.

"No, thank you," Elenore whispered, scurrying off in the direction of the automatic doors.

The noonday sun beamed overhead, temporarily blinding her with its intensity.

She squinted against the brightness and hoisted the groceries up higher in her arms. She had a two mile walk ahead of her, and she needed to hurry if she thought to have dinner ready by the time her father arrived home.

The bags grew heavier the longer Elenore walked, until she thought for sure her arms would fall off.

A truck slowed to a stop beside her. "Need a lift?"

Elenore wanted to say yes, but of course, she didn't. Too many questions would be asked. She'd had her run-in with some of the town folk in the past, which only served to anger her father.

She shook her head and continued on.

"Suit yourself." The truck drove away.

Elenore arrived home approximately forty minutes after leaving the grocery store. Her feet ached almost as much as her arms did.

At least her father wasn't home. For that, she was grateful.

Since Elenore was no longer a minor, the state of Alabama had cut off any financial help Elijah had been receiving after his wife left him twelve years earlier.

He'd been forced to work on a more permanent basis, which afforded Elenore a daily reprieve from his presence. She loved being alone, with no one around but her animals.

Now that Elijah had a little money, he usually spent it on card games and prostitutes, which kept him busy more often than not.

Today would be a "not" day.

After putting the meager amount of groceries away, Elenore tied an apron around her waist and strode out to the chicken coop to gather the eggs.

She shooed the hens aside while attempting to dodge the piles of chicken droppings in her path. If not for the eggs and occasional meat the chickens provided, Elenore would go hungry.

Elijah left thirty dollars on the kitchen counter every Friday. Barely enough to buy the essentials, such as toilet paper and shampoo, let alone bread and canned foods.

So, Elenore had quickly learned how to budget...and shoplift anything she could fit in her pockets.

Once the eggs were gathered, she took out the chicken she'd killed the day before and started dinner.

Elenore had learned at an early age to shut down her emotions and do what had to be done. Besides, she told herself, killing a chicken was essential to her survival. *Nothing more.*

The old clapboard house she shared with her father quickly grew hot after turning on the oven. Even with the windows open, it became stifling. If not for the giant oak trees surrounding the house, she would probably be forced to cook outside.

Elenore wiped at her damp forehead with the back of her hand and switched on the television to watch the local news.

A pretty blonde anchorwoman sat behind a horseshoe-shaped desk, her red lipstick gleaming in the overhead lights. She spoke into the camera. *"Alan Brown makes the third person reported missing in the past two months. All three men are said to be from Haverty County, Alabama."*

Pictures appeared across the screen, with each man's name resting beneath.

Elenore wiped her hands on her apron and moved closer to the television.

"*Hector Gonzalez,*" the anchorwoman continued, "*was last seen nearly eight weeks ago at his place of employment. Dennis Baker went missing approximately a week later. And now, Alan Brown has disappeared. If you have seen or have information on the whereabouts of any of these men, we urge you to contact the Haverty County Sheriff's Department immediately.*"

The sound of a vehicle pulling up out front brought Elenore's head up. Her father was home.

She quickly switched off the television and hurried back to the kitchen to check on the biscuits.

His truck door slammed, filling Elenore with dread. There would be only one reason for his early arrival home... He'd been drinking.

He stomped his way up the back steps to the kitchen and threw open the door. "Elle!"

Elenore could smell the liquor on his breath long before he leaned down and spoke mere inches from her face. "How long before supper?"

She backed up a step. "I—It's almost ready."

His eyes narrowed, his gaze slowly lowering to her chest. "Good. That means we have time for a father-daughter talk."

Elenore swallowed her fear. "T-talk? What would you like to talk about, Daddy?"

"Take it off."

Nausea was instant. "I— The biscuits will burn."

"I don't give a crap about biscuits." He took a step forward, his hand going around to her backside. He squeezed it painfully before jerking her hard against his body. "Do what I said, girl."

Elenore's insides turned cold. There would be no stopping him, no talking him out of what he was about to do. She'd been through it enough times to know what would come next. What always came next.

He released her, spinning her around and shoving her toward the small kitchen table against the opposite wall.

The sound of his belt coming off could be heard over the thundering of her heart.

"Turn around," he slurred.

She couldn't face him for fear she would vomit on him.

He stepped in close behind her, pressing his disgusting erection against her backside. "Turn. Around."

The vomit she fought so hard to hold back shot to her throat, hovering there in the form of bile.

He grabbed a handful of her hair and jerked her head back, his wet, disgusting mouth hovering next to her ear. "You look just like your whore of a mama."

"D-Daddy, p-please," she whispered, knowing without question that begging would do no good. It never did any good.

He twisted her hair tightly in his hold and forced her forward until her face pressed hard against the tabletop.

His free hand yanked up the hem of her dress, tossing it upward around her shoulders.

Her underwear came down next, and then the sound of his sliding zipper echoed throughout the room with haunting finality.

Elenore gripped the edges of the table in preparation of the pain she knew would come.

She bit down on the inside of her lip to keep from crying out, her gaze locked onto the wall in front of her.

She forced her eyes to relax, the sound of the table scraping across the floor beneath her fading to the background. Her vision grew tunneled until her mind slipped into a place that shut out the pain and humiliation of his invasion. A place he couldn't follow. No one could follow...

Chapter Two

Elenore awoke the following morning, her entire body throbbing in pain.

She rolled over in bed to find the sun had already risen.

Panic quickly gripped her. Her father would be up soon, wanting his breakfast.

She tossed the covers back, wincing as she threw her legs over the side of the bed.

The tenderness at the juncture of her thighs was matched only by the pain in her shoulder.

Glancing down, she took in the bruising on her upper arm, the same arm her father had held behind her back as he… She shut down her thoughts, her mind unwilling to recall what had happened to her in that kitchen.

A knock sounded on her door.

Elenore righted her tattered nightgown and surged to her feet.

Her arms instinctively crossed over her chest in anticipation of Elijah's entry.

Odd that he knocked, she thought with more than a little fear, watching intently as the doorknob turned and Elijah stepped into the room.

He stood there, staring at the floor for long moments, and then he extended a cup in her direction. "Thought you might want some orange juice."

Confusion began to mingle with her fear as it always did. The man standing before her now was not the same man who had hurt her yesterday afternoon when he got home.

He took an awkward step forward, still holding that cup in his hand. "Go on, take it."

Elenore hesitantly moved toward him and accepted the cup of juice he held. He'd offered her his juice—a juice she wasn't normally allowed to touch.

He cleared his throat. "Look, Elle. I...um... I'm sorry about yesterday. You know how I get when I've been drinking. I would never hurt you for anything in the world."

More confusion settled in.

"I love you, Elle. I don't know what I would do if you left me like your mama did. I'll stop the drinking this time. I swear it."

Elenore's heart shifted. Her father loved her. That's all she'd ever wanted from him—his love and acceptance.

Part of her loved him in return. But a part, way down deep in her soul, hated the very ground he walked on.

Tears began to gather in her eyes. Maybe he meant it this time? Maybe he realized the monster he became when drinking, and he would finally quit?

She couldn't answer him, so great was the ache in her chest. She ached to be loved, ached to run away and never look back. But mostly, she ached for revenge.

How could she simply forgive him for the pain and humiliation she'd consistently endured at his hands? Hands that should show love and compassion. The very hands he held out to her now.

Elenore took deep, calming breaths, a coping mechanism she'd learned at an early age. She forced her mind to shut out the incomprehensible memories of the day before, set her juice on the nightstand, and moved on wooden legs into her father's outstretched arms.

He gently rocked her, murmuring soothing words above her head that made little sense. "You forgive your ole man?"

She nodded, more out of habit than consent.

"Good girl." He released her and took a step back. "Don't worry about making breakfast for me. I'm going fishing with Dale Mitchell this morning. I'll just grab something on the way."

Elenore stood rooted to the spot long after her father left the room.

Her emotions were all over the place. How could a man who was supposed to love her do the things he did to her? Was it her fault?

She'd come to the conclusion over the years that she was somehow to blame for her mother leaving. And that Mary Griffin's sudden departure was the sole reason her father drank like he did.

Elenore waited until she heard Elijah's truck leave the yard before she stumbled to the bathroom and vomited.

She retched so long and hard her stomach muscles screamed in protest. Yet no matter how much she heaved, she couldn't rid herself of his smell on her.

Staggering to her feet, she turned on the shower, stripped out of her well-worn gown, and stepped under the spray.

She would scrub herself until she bled, if that's what it took to feel clean. But Elenore would never feel clean again. Never.

After her shower, she took down a green dress that had seen better days. But the sleeves were short and the material thin. Which seemed practical given the sweltering heat that was sure to arrive.

She would give anything for a pair of jeans, or pants of any kind, for that matter. But Elijah refused to let her have them. He claimed they were of the devil and reserved for men and… whores.

Slipping on the dress, she moved to stand in front of her mirror. She pulled her long blonde hair back into a ponytail and stared at her reflection. She really did resemble her mother.

Resentment boiled up inside her, the longer she stood there, looking at herself. *That is what Daddy sees when he looks at me,* she thought with more than a little disgust. *Mother.*

An image of Mary Griffin's crying face suddenly flashed through Elenore's mind. *"Elijah, don't!"*

A whimper escaped Elenore. She staggered back a few steps, her hand flying to her mouth.

The memory of Mary trying desperately to protect her daughter didn't add up with the tales Elenore had been told all her life. Even though the stories came from Elijah, Elenore had no reason not to believe him. Why else would her mother have left her behind?

According to Elijah, Mary had run off with a friend of his when Elenore was eight years old.

She'd never returned or attempted to contact her daughter in the last twelve years.

Elenore hated herself in that moment more than she'd ever hated herself before. Something was wrong with her, something bad enough that her own mother hadn't wanted her. And though her father had never walked away from her, he blamed her for her mother leaving. Elenore could see it in his eyes. Especially when he drank.

Titles by Ditter Kellen

Elle Series

I am Elle - A Psychological Thriller

Elle Returns: The Sequel – Book 2

Elle Unleashed – Book 3

The Boy in the Window

A Suspense Thriller

The Girl Named Mud

A Gripping Suspense Novel

The Girl Who Lived to Tell

A Chilling Psychological Thriller

Where Corn Don't Grow

Psychological Thriller – Coming Soon

Quick Chronicles

A Psychological Thriller Series

The Silencer – Book 1

The Prophet – Book 2 - Releasing early 2020

The Hitcher

A Bone-Chilling Psychological Thriller

About Ditter

Ditter Kellen is the USA Today Bestselling Author of Mystery/Thriller/Suspense/Crime Fiction Novels. She loves spinning edgy, heart-pounding mysteries that will leave you guessing until the very end. That includes psychological thrillers with a touch of horror, as well as family drama laced with murder and jaw dropping scenes, some might find difficult to read.

Ditter resides in Alabama with her husband and many unique farm animals. She adores French fries and her phone is permanently attached to her ear. You can contact Ditter by email: Ditterkellen@outlook.com

Made in the USA
Middletown, DE
22 April 2020

90878990R00225